# Memories of You

# Also From J. Kenner

**Fallen Saint Series:**
My Fallen Saint
My Beautiful Sin
My Cruel Salvation

**Stark Security:**
Shattered With You
Broken With You
Ruined With You
Wrecked With You
Destroyed With You
Ravaged With You

**The Stark Saga:**
Release Me
Claim Me
Complete Me
Anchor Me
Lost With Me
Damien
Enchant Me

**Stark Ever After:**
Take Me
Have Me
Play My Game
Seduce Me
Unwrap Me
Deepest Kiss
Entice Me
Hold Me
Please Me
Indulge Me
Delight Me
Cherish Me
Embrace Me

All Night Long
In Too Deep
Light My Fire
Walk The Line
Royal Cocktail
Bar Bites: A Man of the Month Cookbook

**Blackwell-Lyon:**
Lovely Little Liar
Pretty Little Player
Sexy Little Sinner
Tempting Little Tease

Also by Julie Kenner

**Demon Hunting Soccer Mom Series:**
Carpe Demon
California Demon
Demons Are Forever
Deja Demon
The Demon You Know
Demon Ex Machina
Pax Demonica

**The Dark Pleasures Series:**
Caress of Darkness
Find Me in Darkness
Find Me in Pleasure
Find Me in Passion
Caress of Pleasure

**Rising Storm:**
Tempest Rising
Quiet Storm

# Memories of You

A Stark Security Novella

## By J. Kenner

1001 DARK NIGHTS
PRESS

Memories of You
A Stark Security Novella
By J. Kenner

Copyright 2021 Julie Kenner
ISBN: 978-1-951812-55-3

Published by 1001 Dark Nights Press, an imprint of Evil Eye Concepts, Incorporated

Sign up for the 1001 Dark Nights Newsletter
and be entered to win a Tiffany Key necklace.

There's a contest every month!

Go to www.1001DarkNights.com to subscribe.

**As a bonus, all subscribers can download
FIVE FREE exclusive books!**

# Acknowledgments from the Author

Special thanks to Liz Berry who pointed out that Abby really needed a story!

# One Thousand and One Dark Nights

*Once upon a time, in the future…*

*I was a student fascinated with stories and learning.
I studied philosophy, poetry, history, the occult, and
the art and science of love and magic. I had a vast
library at my father's home and collected thousands
of volumes of fantastic tales.*

*I learned all about ancient races and bygone
times. About myths and legends and dreams of all
people through the millennium. And the more I read
the stronger my imagination grew until I discovered
that I was able to travel into the stories… to actually
become part of them.*

*I wish I could say that I listened to my teacher
and respected my gift, as I ought to have. If I had, I
would not be telling you this tale now.
But I was foolhardy and confused, showing off
with bravery.*

*One afternoon, curious about the myth of the
Arabian Nights, I traveled back to ancient Persia to
see for myself if it was true that every day Shahryar
(Persian: شهریار, "king") married a new virgin, and then
sent yesterday's wife to be beheaded. It was written
and I had read that by the time he met Scheherazade,
the vizier's daughter, he'd killed one thousand
women.*

*Something went wrong with my efforts. I arrived in the midst of the story and somehow exchanged places with Scheherazade – a phenomena that had never occurred before and that still to this day, I cannot explain.*

*Now I am trapped in that ancient past. I have taken on Scheherazade's life and the only way I can protect myself and stay alive is to do what she did to protect herself and stay alive.*

*Every night the King calls for me and listens as I spin tales. And when the evening ends and dawn breaks, I stop at a point that leaves him breathless and yearning for more. And so the King spares my life for one more day, so that he might hear the rest of my dark tale.*

*As soon as I finish a story... I begin a new one... like the one that you, dear reader, have before you now.*

# Prologue

*He lives there in my earliest memories. The boy next door with his quick smile and stupid jokes. We'd play tag in the cul-de-sac with his brother and the neighborhood kids. We'd look for rocks in the field behind our house, getting filthy, then splashing in the blow-up pool to wash off the grime. He was my best friend, my closest ally, the boy with whom I shared all my secrets.*

*He was my rock before he became my crush, the boy about whom I drew hearts on my notebook and wrote long passages in my diary. I never told him, though. I never shared that part of my heart. His friendship meant too much, and we clung to it like brother and sister over the years.*

*My heart broke for him when his family shattered.*

*That horrible D word.*

*Divorce.*

*Then he was gone. His father to one coast, and his mother to another, taking the boy I adored and his brother with her. I mourned the loss, even more so when we lost touch.*

*And though life went on, I can't deny that he left a hole in my heart.*

*Now he's back, and this time a wild passion crackles between us, filling me with hope and promise.*

*But I can see how the years have broken him, and now I can't help but fear that the boy I always needed has grown into a man I can never have.*

# Chapter One

"I'm being paranoid," I say as I walk down Wilshire toward Java B's, a local Los Angeles coffee house that recently opened up in Santa Monica, right near my new office. "They were probably just wrong numbers, right?"

"Sure, Abby," Lilah says, the sarcasm coming through my earbuds loud and clear. "Because that's what people who dial a wrong number do. They don't just hang up. They stay on the line and mouth breathe like the low-life cretins they are. And then they call a zillion more times in a two-day period."

It's a typical Lilah answer, and even though she's right—I'm probably dealing with an actual creep and not a wrong number—it makes me feel better.

I ask her to hang on as I head into the coffee shop and get in line to order. She starts humming the theme from *Jeopardy*, and I roll my eyes and ignore her as I wait for my turn to order.

I met Lilah Barrett on the first day of my sophomore year of high school. I'd been working up the courage to tell Renly Cooper, my childhood bestie, that freshman year had been hell because I'd developed a huge crush on him. And rather than just deal with it, I'd avoided him. Not that he'd noticed. He'd been too into sports and debate and theater, whereas I was the tech geek who hung out in the STEM wing and wrote computer games instead of doing my homework.

I'd been hoping to man up and let him know that I missed hanging out with him, and that even though we didn't live next door to each other anymore, that I was hoping we could still be friends. I wasn't sure if I was going to own up to my crush, but Renly always had a knack for reading my mind, so I figured he probably already knew that part.

I was nervous as shit, just standing there waiting by his locker, when this fairy-like wraith of a girl came up and started fiddling with the combination lock.

"Um, are you getting something for Renly?" I'd asked.

She'd turned pale blue eyes on me, then said, "Wow, there's a lot of orange in your aura. What's stressing you out?"

I should have said it was none of her business.

I should have asked why she was getting into his locker.

Instead, I word vomited my life onto her, ending with the fact that I was waiting for Renly to basically tell him that my teenage hormones were under control and that I missed my bestie.

"Oh, wow. That really blows. Maybe you can track down his new phone number and tell him? Hanging on to that kind of emo baggage can really mess with your aura, and yours is already funky."

I ignored the aura bit but dove straight to the heart of the matter. "New phone number?"

She shrugged. "They told me at the office that the guy assigned to this locker moved out of town. So I guess it's mine until graduation. Sorry about that."

Renly and Red had been doing the Divorced Parent Dance that summer, pushed off to stay with their dad up north, even though they didn't want to go. It turns out that while they were away, their mom had pulled up stakes and moved herself and the boys down to Houston, which meant I hadn't seen him since he'd left in June.

The whole situation sucked, but at least it meant that I didn't have to pretend to be over my crush when I was around him. Not exactly a plus considering I was still missing my friend.

The upside was that I gained Lilah. And despite the fact that we're so different—or maybe because of it—she fast became one of my closest friends.

Now we're neighbors, too, as I rent half of a Santa Monica duplex that she inherited from her parents after they died in a helicopter crash our first year at UCLA.

"A latte?" she says once I'm back on the street. "I thought you were cutting down on caffeine."

"No, you said I should cut down on caffeine. And I said I'd try. Today, I need frothy, caffeinated comfort." I take a sip and sigh with pleasure. Then I frown when I remember why I need comfort in the first place.

"How many calls today?" she asks.

"Seven today. Five yesterday."

"Do you think it has to do with Fuck Me Now?"

I hold back a snort. "That is not what the app is called, and you know it."

"Hey, I just believe in truth in advertising."

"That's not what I'm looking for, and you know that too. I had that. It wasn't what I wanted, and I wouldn't sign up for that kind of app." I know I sound frustrated, but it's only because I am. It's just so damn hard to meet anybody in this town, and I'm not interested in serial hookups or even friends with benefits."

"You're right, you're right. I'm sorry. Back to the topic. Do you think it has anything to do with Tribe Find?"

"I don't know. Maybe?" About a month ago, I decided to try out a new friend and dating app that a guy I knew in college recently rolled out. You can use it to look for new friends—finding your tribe—or to set up dates. It's supposed to be focused on relationships, not hookups, and while online dating was never my thing, since Cedric created it, I agreed to be a beta user.

"Do folks on the app have your phone number?"

"No," I say. "The app does, but it's not shared. But the calls are coming to my work phone, too. Those are the ones I answer. I let unknown calls on my cell roll to voicemail."

"You're getting them both places?"

"Yup."

"You went out on a couple of dates through the app, right?"

"Yeah, I—oh, hold on. It's Darrin."

I put Lilah on hold, then take the incoming call. Darrin is a new hire at the LA office of Greystone-Branch Consulting, Fairchild & Partners Development's biggest client. And since I am the partner in "Partners," I put on my office voice and take the call.

"Darrin, I'm not at my desk anymore. Did we forget something?" It's past six on Friday, and I spent most of the morning and afternoon on a video call with him as we worked through various features they want added into some new marketing software we're designing. The walk to get coffee was to clear my head before I take my laptop home, spread work out on my kitchen table, and dive into my backlog.

Yeah, I know how to start the weekend with a bang.

"No, no. I think we got a great start. There's a lot to do, though, and Bijan is breathing down my neck. I was thinking I could meet you at your office tomorrow? Might be more efficient. Assuming that doesn't mess up your weekend."

"No, no, not at all." *Damn, damn, damn.* I *do* plan to work tomorrow, but I'd intended to do it from home. Still, client relationships are important, and he's right that we're running tight on time. "How about we meet at two? I have to take care of some things in the morning."

"Perfect," he says. "And I appreciate it. I'm still new, and this is my first project to shepherd through from start to finish. I want to impress the boss, you know?"

I laugh. "Yeah. I know." I feel the same way about my boss—correction, *partner.* Nikki Fairchild Stark is brilliant at tech and coding and relentless in getting a job done right. She's also great with clients, drop dead pretty, and married to billionaire Damien Stark. I should be intimidated as hell, and I was in the early days. Now she's become a truly close friend.

"Important?" Lilah asks when I come back on the line.

"He's nervous about the deadline. I don't blame him. There was that one guy," I continue, shifting back to the creepy guy topic. "He kept telling me I was pretty and then wanted to chat about retro computer games. I mean, he was nice enough, just kinda awkward, but maybe..."

"Maybe it is him, and it's not nefarious at all. Maybe he's trying to work up the courage to talk to you."

"Maybe..." It doesn't feel right, though, and I tell her so.

"Travis?"

"No way," I say. "It got weird between us, but he wouldn't—"

"Just tossing out ideas. And you know what I think about his aura."

I frown. A former co-worker who quit about a month ago, Travis and I went out a couple of times. I'd thought he wanted to date. He thought we just wanted to fool around. It was rough for a while, but we worked it out. "We're still friends," I say. "And his aura is fine. Besides, he's in Orange County. If he was obsessed with me, he'd have hung around."

"Maybe," she concedes. "But that leaves us back at the app. It's probably some guy who figured out who you were from your profile picture and is bummed because you didn't pick him from the masses. Or another one of the guys you went out for drinks with. We can rule out retro game boy, but did any of the others seem the stalky type?"

I consider that. "Not really."

"Hmm. Well, maybe you should reach out to them anyway. See if any of them acts all shifty-eyed."

I make a face. The last thing I want to do is to reach out to guys I didn't hit it off with as friends or romantic partners. "I'm thinking about opting for the *ignore it and it will go away* plan."

To her credit, she laughs. "Well, that's one way. And honestly, I wouldn't worry too much. It's just some asshole. How dangerous can a mouth breather be?"

Since I'm a huge horror movie fan, I don't answer. But the sound of Michael Myers breathing immediately starts to play in my head. *Great.*

"Let's continue this at home tonight. Cocktails on the porch?"

"Definitely," I say, and we end the call.

Since my laptop is already in my tote, I don't have to head back inside. Instead, I go straight to my car, which is parked on the street. Usually I park in the garage, but I'd popped out in the afternoon and there was a spot right there, so I grabbed it. Now I'm coming up on the rear of the cute little blue Fiat I bought when Nikki made me a partner.

I veer to the left toward the driver's side, then slow, because something isn't right. It takes a second for my mind to catch up with reality, but once I've reached the driver's side door, there's no escaping the truth.

My knees go weak, and I reach out, grabbing the side of the car to keep from falling. Because the hood of my car is covered in something viscous and red, and I'm pretty damn sure that it's blood.

# Chapter Two

Renly Cooper leaned back against the desk that he'd been assigned when he joined Stark Security a few weeks ago. Honestly, it seemed longer. For the first time in a long time, he felt as if he'd found a home. A purpose.

And God knew a guy like him needed purpose in his work, because he sure as hell wasn't mining it from his personal life.

From across the room, Linda Starr waved at him, then motioned for him to come join. He grinned, then nodded as he pushed off the desk. He'd only recently met Linda and her husband—or rather her ex-husband-soon-to-be-husband again—but he'd taken an instant liking to both of them. Hell, to everyone on the team.

He only hoped he could live up to their expectations of him. He'd been honest with Damien Stark and Ryan Hunter about the injury that had caused him to leave the SEALs, but he'd been a little vague on the details. The truth was, they wanted someone with Hollywood connections, and he'd wanted a job with a bit more gravitas. Now he was looking forward to escaping the Hollywood spotlight and taking some of the international assignments that he knew were becoming more and more frequent for the growing agency.

"You're looking happy," Linda said. "I hope that means I'm going to enjoy it here, too. Us newbies need to stick together."

"I'm pretty sure this is the kind of job I was born for," he said honestly. "Solid tactical and investigative operations on a global scale. It'll be a nice change from working on movie sets."

"A big change from your SEAL work for sure, but it must have been interesting."

"It was," he admitted. "But I want to be in the field. Not helping choreograph a fictional version of the field."

She tilted her head, her eyes narrowing as if he was a puzzle she couldn't figure out. "So why'd you do it in the first place?"

He grimaced. "Long story," he said, which was technically true. "I'll lay it out for you one day. I didn't hate it—not by a long shot. And I met lots of interesting people."

She trilled a laugh. "Yeah, the whole town's seen pictures of you and those interesting people."

"Yeah, well—"

She waved his words away. "I'm just giving you grief. Sorry. Bottom line is you liked it, but it wasn't what you were made to do."

"Exactly."

"Then it's good you're here. Nice to have another freshman in the class. And your Hollywood connections are handy, right? I mean, you got me and Winston into that party."

He chuckled. "Yes, I did." He'd dated superstar Francesca Muratti longer than he should have, and her guilty pleasure was to go to *those kinds* of clubs and show just enough skin as she exited the limo that the inevitable tabloid reporters couldn't resist publishing the pictures. She'd leave the really kinky stuff to the private rooms, but she knew how to get press, even if it wasn't the kind of press Renly liked.

"I'm glad that worked out for you," he added. She and Winston had gone into the sex party together as part of an operation, but he knew damn well they'd had issues of their own to work on, too.

The corner of her mouth twitched. "Oh, it did. For the case and for the two of us. Always nice to reconnect with the one you love, you know?" She nodded toward Winston, her expression a mixture of softness laced with heat.

"Yeah," he lied. "I know."

"Speaking of," she continued, "I'm going to go mingle with him. I just wanted to say that I'm glad we'll be working together."

"Me too," he said sincerely. In truth, there wasn't anyone at Stark Security who wasn't completely up to snuff. Except possibly him.

He drew in a breath, squared his shoulders, and ordered himself to get the hell over it. Then he let his gaze roam the room.

The workday was wrapping up, but everyone in town was in the office, along with a few spouses and friends, and all to welcome Linda to the fold. He'd had a similar welcome gathering when he'd officially joined the team, but Linda's had an energy that his party hadn't, primarily because the circumstances of her arrival at Stark Security were so unusual, what with the fact that—until a few weeks ago—her husband, Winston, had believed she was dead.

So it was a celebration of not only her new job, but her renewed life. And love, too. Because as he watched the two of them together— the heated glances, the shared smiles—it was clear that those two were meant for each other.

That's what it looked like, anyway. But Renly had worked long enough in Hollywood to know that things weren't always as they seemed.

Hollywood? Hell, his own life was a study in things not being what they seemed. Or at least his life was concrete support for the adage that good things never last.

He hoped Winston and Linda were the exception to that rule. He really did.

"Renly?"

He blinked, then realized that he'd been staring at the couple, Linda's hand tucked into Winston's, her expression so full of love it made his heart ache. "Sorry," he said. "I feel like a voyeur."

They both laughed, and he mentally kicked himself as he turned toward Nikki Stark, who was standing right by the couple. Talk about an exception. As far as Renly could tell, Nikki and Damien Stark weren't just in the top one percent for wealth, but also for passion. God knew those two had been through a lot, all played out in the tabloids, and they were still—

"Sorry," Nikki said, the word interrupting his thoughts as she caught Linda's eye. "There's an emergency. I need to run."

Winston stepped toward her. "The kids?"

She shook her head as her eyes scanned the room, presumably for Damien. "No. No, it's my assistant. Sorry. I mean my partner."

Renly frowned as that tidbit clicked into place. "Abby?" He took a step forward. "Is she okay?"

A few days before, he'd learned that his childhood friend, Abigail Jones, worked with Nikki. He'd planned to look her up right away, but he'd been busy following up on a corporate espionage investigation with Leah and just hadn't done it yet. That and the fact that he treasured the memory of the friendship they'd had in their youth, and he didn't want it to be tainted by the very real likelihood that they no longer clicked.

Nikki frowned at her phone and then looked up at him. "I—I...

I'm not sure." She swallowed, fear shadowing her lovely face. "Sorry. I really need to run," Nikki continued, lifting her hand to catch Damien's attention.

"Of course," Winston said as she started to pass.

Renly didn't even hesitate. This was Abby, after all. "Wait," he said. "I'm coming with you."

\* \* \* \*

Renly raced to the scene behind Nikki and Damien, the rumble and roar of his 2019 Ducati Panigale surrounding him. The sound was loud, almost numbing, but it damn sure wasn't enough to erase the worry that was crawling through him like a parasite.

*What the hell had happened to Abby?*

He wished he'd asked for the address. Damien Stark knew how to handle that Bugatti, and he was definitely pushing the speed limit, but Renly would have left him in the dust by now if he only knew where they were going.

One turn, then another, and too many damn stoplights, and all the while his mind was spinning with fear.

In the end, the ride took less than ten minutes, but it felt like an eternity. Then, when he saw her standing there by a little blue Fiat that was so very Abby, he actually had to take a moment to breathe, shocked by not only the intensity of his relief, but also by the flood of joy that burst through him simply from seeing her again.

Nikki was already at her side, having tumbled out of the Bugatti the moment it stopped, and Damien was just a few steps away.

Renly, however, felt frozen.

*She was okay.*

He let the words roll over him, shocked by his intense visceral reaction, though he knew he shouldn't be. Abby had been his rock when his mother had lost her hearing, and then again when his father had packed up and moved out, hauling his ass to New York.

So yeah. Abby was important to him. Of course he was relieved.

He was also stalling, he realized, though he wasn't sure why.

Except, of course, that was a lie. It had been over a decade since they'd seen each other, and yet he would have recognized her anywhere. Her wide eyes and blond curls. That sweet mouth that he remembered in a smile but was now curved into a frown as her teeth worried her lower lip.

Over the years he'd gone so far as to pick up the phone to call her, only to put it down again when he realized that he was calling because there was shit in his life he wanted to talk through—and why the hell would he think she'd appreciate him dumping that in her lap without even a Christmas card during the passing years?

She'd remained in his mind and his heart, the only close female friend he'd ever had in his life. Even Tascha, who'd gone side by side with him into combat and for whom he'd put his life on the line, had never gotten close enough to see the childhood demons that had formed the man. And that still tormented him.

Abby had, and maybe it made him a damn pussy, but if she didn't recognize him, it was going to be like a goddamn knife to the heart.

*Fuck it.*

He got off the bike and hurried toward them, pulling off his helmet as he went. Abby was shaking her head, hovering near the driver's door as Nikki said something soothing.

Then she stopped, her head turning as her eyes went wide. Then she squealed and sprinted toward him, her arms wide as she threw herself at him, crying out, *"Renly!"*

He caught her and spun her around, all the time feeling like a damn idiot. This was Abby, after all.

So what the hell had he been worried about?

# Chapter Three

"Renly Cooper, is it really you?" I'm breathing hard, unsteady on my feet now that he's put me down. I'm dizzy, yes, but not because he's spun me around. No, I'm unsteady because the whole freaking earth is shifting on its axis. "When the hell did you grow up?"

*And grow up so fine, too,* though I don't say that last part out loud. The Renly I used to know wouldn't care, but I'm not certain about this gorgeous action-hero of a male specimen. I mean, the youthful, athletic guy I knew was seriously cute, but the Renly in front of me is the kind of man women drool over.

I brush the back of my hand over my mouth—just to check—then laugh as I shake my head. Considering I was literally freaking out and terrified not ten minutes ago, I have to say I'm feeling pretty darn good. "You have made my entire day," I tell him. "I mean, you have *completely* turned it around."

He's grinning, too. "So are you finished? She always did talk too much," he adds with a quick glance toward Damien.

I smack him lightly on the shoulder. "I'm too giddy to berate you for teasing me," I say. "How are you even here?"

"I took the wrong left turn," he says, alluding to our own private joke—one that started in fourth grade, though I don't remember how, and we both start laughing again.

Beside us, Nikki clears her throat, clearly fighting a laugh of her own. I see her glance toward Damien, who reaches for her hand before speaking. "I'm going to go out on a limb and assume you two know each other?"

I meet Renly's eyes, then shrug. "Nope."

"Never seen her before in my life," he adds. He glances between the two of them, then turns back to me. "I don't think they believe us."

"Yeah, well, Damien's pretty sharp. He doesn't miss much."

"Thanks a lot," Nikki says, and I flash my boss—my *partner*—a happy grin. This day has done a complete one-eighty.

"We grew up next door to each other," Renly explains. "We made a pact in fourth grade. Me and Abby."

"Poor Red," I say.

"I have to second that," Nikki says. "I'm definitely Team Red."

I look between the two of them, the pieces falling together. "Wait, you're saying that the guy named Red who helped you during the hostage thing in Manhattan was Red *Cooper*?"

"We were all three friends," Renly continues, "but Abs and I were practically joined at the hip, especially in junior high." Renly meets my eyes again. "Red is going to have a cow when he hears you're in town."

"Red's here?" Now my head is really spinning. Red and Renly both in the LA area? "How did I not know any of this?"

It's a rhetorical question; I know perfectly well what happened. We'd lost track after his mom dragged them all the way from the Santa Clarita Valley to Houston. And, to be painfully honest, we'd started to drift apart even before that, a sad fact for which I blame myself since by that time I'd developed an honest-to-goodness crush on him. And, of course, was avoiding him completely.

It wasn't hard. I was a techie hanging out in the STEM wing, and he was suddenly ridiculously popular, what with the athletics and his seriously awesome looks. Which, of course, means he barely noticed how little I was around. After all, he practically had a harem of girls who'd matured a hell of a lot faster than me.

If I sound bitter, it's only because I was. At the time I blamed him. Now I know I was a shitty friend.

Maybe we would've found our footing again, but then they left for Texas. After that, we had a few calls and emails during high school, then just sort of lost touch. I knew that Renly had joined the military, but once I got sucked into college and work, I lost complete track of him.

Of course, he lost track of me as well.

Right now, though, none of that matters. I'm too happy to see him again. This boy who'd been my best friend and my first crush.

"—but what the hell is going on?"

I realize I've gotten completely lost in my own thoughts, and I blink up at him. "What?"

Renly's expression is part concern, part exasperation. "Nikki said there was an emergency—that you were in trouble."

"Oh!" I whip my head around to Nikki and Damien, who've completely flown from my mind, not to mention the mess on my car that is what had made me call Nikki in the first place.

"No, no." I shake my head. "It's okay. I realized after I called that it's okay. Weird, but not as scary as I'd thought. When you pulled up, I was telling Nikki and Damien that I'd cried wolf too early."

"And I was pointing out that just because it's fake doesn't mean it wasn't intentional," Nikki says, her mouth curved down into a frown.

"Fake?" Renly repeats. "Fake what?" He moves over, shifting his angle enough so that he can see the hood of my car. I follow him, grimacing when I see it again. The horrible mess of red goo smeared all over the hood. "What the hell?" he says, his voice low and dangerous.

"I saw it and freaked," I explain. "I've been getting these weird calls with hang-ups and so I was on edge. I thought it was blood, and I overreacted."

"It *is* blood," Renly says, moving closer and then dragging his finger through the goo. "Of a sort, anyway. Corn syrup, dye, a little soap. A few other ingredients. All adds up to the kind of fake blood they use on film sets." He turns back to me with a grimace. "Guess whoever's harassing you didn't have the stomach to actually sacrifice a goat on your hood."

I cringe, then hug myself, my joy at seeing Renly fading in the knowledge that somebody had at the very least, wanted me to think it was blood.

"It's not just your car," Damien says from a few yards away. I hadn't realized he'd stepped away, but now he's walking back toward us along the row of cars parked parallel to the sidewalk. "Two of the cars between you and the intersection have the same stuff on their hoods."

Hope flutters in my chest. "So this wasn't about me? I don't need to worry?"

"I want to hear more about these calls," Renly says firmly. "But if there's only been a few hangups and no escalation, then you're probably okay. The question is—is this goo an escalation?"

"I'd be more concerned if it was only your car. Or real blood," Nikki says as Damien frowns at his phone screen. "The fact that it's fake already has me feeling less worried. And now that we know you're not the only one, it doesn't really feel like you're a target." She looks at

Renly. "What do you think?"

"Probably someone filming a movie nearby," he says. "Something low budget, with a volunteer PA who decided to get their jollies on after the filming."

I look at Renly. "Wow. That's very specific."

He shrugs. "I've been doing a lot of work on movie sets these days. I've seen a lot of the interns, and I know how college kids can be. Especially if one of them is trying to impress their friends. It wouldn't happen on a big budget action movie, but someone from one of the film schools doing a short film that needed some fake blood? I can see some idiot on the crew spreading it around a few cars just for kicks and grins."

"Good call," Damien says. "There's a student crew from UCLA about three blocks over filming a horror movie. One of their buckets of fake blood was stolen last night."

"How do you know—"

He grins at Nikki. "I texted Rachel," he says, referring to his executive assistant. "She called the local precinct. The supervising professor reported it. Some folding tables and equipment were also pinched."

"So it's just some kid screwing around," I say, relief sweeping through me.

"Probably," Renly says. "To be sure, we'll pull the video footage." He glances at our office building and the others nearby. "I'm not sure any of the security cameras have a street view, but it's worth checking. I'll ask Ryan to put someone on it."

"Perfect," Damien says as I do yet another mental reset.

"Wait," I say to Renly. "Ryan? Does that mean you're…" I trail off, looking from him to Damien and then back to Renly again. "Holy crap, that's why you were with Nikki? You're working at Stark Security?"

"Renly's the second newest member of the team," Damien adds. "He joined right before Winston went off to Texas to find out how his dead wife had come back to life."

I grimace. I don't work at Stark Security, the agency founded by Damien after the kidnapping of his youngest daughter. But I hear stories from Nikki, and the one about Winston Starr learning that the wife he'd believed dead from a car bomb was actually an assassin who'd faked her death was the kind of story that could be a movie. Fake blood and all.

But it's not Winston and Linda's story that's making my head spin, and I twirl my finger as I focus on Renly. "Let's rewind, shall we?" I look between the three of them. "You're working at Stark Security? I thought you were off in the Middle East doing SEAL stuff."

"You knew that?" His brows go up, and it's clear he's surprised.

I lift my shoulders in a shrug. "I ask my mom about you every once in a while. She doesn't know much, but she hears things from your mom. They've stayed in touch. A little, anyway."

"Well, she's behind the times. I didn't re-up. And I've been in LA for almost two years now. I thought you'd gone up north to MIT after doing time at UCLA."

"And after graduation, I came back here and I ended up—" I cut myself off. "You know what? I think we have a *lot* of catching up to do. I've got a place not that far away. Do you want to come over? Have some wine and swap stories?"

I glance at Nikki and Damien. "You two are welcome, too, of course. I am so grateful that you came to my rescue, and I'm so sorry that it was a false alarm." I make a face. "And I really need to run through a car wash before that stuff destroys my paint."

Nikki laughs. "Do *not* be sorry that it was a false alarm, and thank you for the invite. But I think we'll go back to the party and let everyone know you're fine."

"You're sure? I mean, shouldn't Renly be there?"

"I don't think Linda or Winston will mind," Renly says.

"They won't," Damien says. "And although this whole thing is probably going to turn out to be just a few prank calls, I'm going to call it right now and say that Renly's officially assigned to keep you safe. Okay by you, Cooper?"

"Hell yes," Renly says.

"But—" I begin but am cut off by his hand in the air.

"It's my job. And I wanted to make sure you got home safe, anyway. And," he adds with that same smile that turned me to goo during The Renly Crush years, "we really do have a whole lot of catching up to do."

# Chapter Four

I head toward a self-serve car wash not far from my place, and he follows me there on his bike. I keep sneaking looks at him in the rearview mirror as we drive, still not completely able to believe that Renly's back in my life.

The thought brings me up short, and I wonder if he really is. Back, I mean. After all, while our few moments on the street were full of excitement and adrenaline, it may turn out that we don't have a single thing in common. He may end up at my house, and all we'll have between us is some horrible, lingering silence.

Dear God, I hope not. Because right now, I'm buzzing with happiness from seeing him again. And I really don't want that feeling to end.

I turn into the car wash lot, then pull into one of the little stalls. I take a deep breath before I kill the engine to center myself. No matter what happens, it's good to reconnect with him. And so long as I keep reminding myself of that, everything will be fine. It's all about managing expectations, after all, and I do that every single day with clients.

In the rearview mirror, I watch as he gets off the bike, then walks toward me across the lot. I get out and meet him at the rear of the car.

"I haven't got a single quarter," he says. "Do you?"

I laugh. "Not a one. But I do have a credit card." I'm about to walk over to that side and start the system running, but he gets there first, sliding in his card and then grinning at me as the machinery starts rumbling.

This particular car wash has a hose on each side of the stall. I've always assumed that was so that you don't have to drag a dirty hose over your newly cleaned half in order to wash the other side. Now I consider another purpose.

Renly apparently has the same thought, because I see the gleam in his eyes as he goes to the far side, then grabs the coiled hose, his hand poised on the nozzle.

"Don't you even think about it," I say, going for my own hose.

His eyes widen, all innocent and guileless. "I don't know what you're talking about."

I burst out laughing. Then, still laughing, I pull the trigger on my own hose and spray him, accidentally getting him full-on in the crotch.

"Seriously?" he says. "Sweetheart, you are so going to pay for that."

"Phhbbt." I dance away from the spray he aims at me. "I would have thought someone in the military would have a faster reaction time."

He aims again, and this time manages to completely soak the T-shirt I'd worn to work this morning. "Hey!" I protest. "This is a genuine discount bin Old Navy T-shirt. How dare you defile it?"

"Well, it fits you very nicely," he says, letting his eyes skim over me in what I know is an exaggerated leer.

I glance down, realizing that since I knew I was going to be the only one in the office today, I hadn't bothered to wear a bra. That's something I can usually get away with, but in a wet T-shirt, even my barely-B-cup breasts look pretty perky.

I roll my eyes. "Perv."

"I apologize for nothing."

"Behave," I order, then point to the Fiat's hood. "And clean."

He does, this time aiming the spray so that it doesn't splash goo on me. I join in from my side, and soon enough we've not only eradicated the fake blood but have thoroughly cleaned the entire car.

He steps back, looking it over like a foreman on an assembly line before meeting my eyes over the roof. "Do you remember all those times we'd run around in your backyard, me with the hose from the back of the house, and you with the one from the side?"

"I nailed you almost every time," I say.

"Like hell you did. I let you get away with it. I'm a year older than you, remember? I had to watch over you. Be careful not to bruise that fragile child's confidence."

I make a face. "A week," I say. "Our birthdays are only one week apart." December and January, true, but still only a week.

"It is what it is. Two different years. I'm clearly older and wiser."

"Wiseass, I think you mean."

"Well, that's true enough," he says, then shakes his head.

"What?"

"I just…I just can't believe it's been so long since we talked."

My whole body seems to go soft. "I know. Me too."

For a moment, silence lingers. Then, just before it gets weird, I clear my throat. "Right," I say. "So, um, we should probably get to my house. I could use some dry clothes." I grimace. "I'm sorry I sprayed you. I didn't even think about the fact that you probably don't keep a change of clothes folded up somewhere on your bike."

"If you have a dryer, I think we'll be just fine."

"Right," I say, trying not to blush as I think about what he's going to wear as his clothes are spinning. "I'm a full-service hostess. I'll even wash them for you if you want."

"I never turn down a free wash," he says with such mock seriousness I start laughing all over again.

I get myself under control, then clear my throat. "Okay, let's go."

He takes a step, then stumbles. He reaches out, steadying himself with a hand on the hood of my car as I hurry that way. "Are you okay?"

He holds up a hand. "Yeah. Yeah, I just slipped on some leftover stuff on the ground."

He glances toward his bike, then back at me. "Why don't I ride with you and get it tomorrow or later tonight?"

"Um, yeah, if you're sure." I nod to the car. "Hop on in."

It's not far to my place, and I score a spot right in front of the duplex. It's probably just as well that he left his bike at the car wash since parking on my street requires a permit. Besides, I know the car wash's owner and he won't mind. In fact, I send him a text just to let him know.

We get out, and right away I see Lilah sitting on the front porch, watching us with an eagle eye. It's a friendly neighborhood, and Lilah and I like to drink wine on the shared front porch and chat with the neighbors. Especially the forty-something TV writer who moved in across the street and has completely captured Lilah's imagination. So I'm not surprised to see her on the porch now, especially since we'd planned to do that very thing tonight.

"Look at you," she calls as we get out of the car. "Bringing home random men?"

"Ha ha," I say. "Lilah, meet Renly." I keep my eyes on her face to watch her reaction. I'm immediately rewarded, and she actually stands up, pushing herself out of the chair as if in reflex.

"Empty locker Renly?"

"Yup." I turn to face Renly directly. "I know Lilah because of you," I say. "Lilah, Renly. Renly, Lilah."

"I inherited your locker," Lilah tells him. She holds out her hand to shake his as we reach the porch. "You kept it clean. There was no sweaty boy smell at all."

"Well, I'm glad to hear that, but I have a feeling that's more to do with the janitorial staff than me. I was definitely a sweaty boy back then."

She looks at me, then grins. "He's got a good aura," she says, then adds, "I would tell you to come out and sit with me and have some wine so I can interrogate you both about your childhood, but I have to blow off tonight's drinking session. Turns out that I have a date."

"Really?"

"Yep. With a charming little man who has a thing about clownfish."

I laugh. "Babysitting?"

"All night. My cousin and her husband are doing their anniversary at a hotel. So be as loud as you want," she adds with a sly look at Renly.

She lowers her voice, as if whispering a secret. "Abby's bedroom shares a wall with my living room."

To his credit, Renly barely reacts, but I see the way his eyes brighten with humor, and the corner of his lip twitches. I shake my head as if in exasperation. "Lilah. You know we're just friends. Like friend friends."

"Friends with benefits. It's the only way to go. Way less messy than a relationship."

I shake my head, then glance sideways at Renly. "Lilah's a great friend and I love her, but if you want to demonstrate how you can kill her with your bare hands I won't hold it against you." I shift my attention back to Lilah. "All that SEAL training, you know."

"And that's my cue," she says. "Seriously, you two have fun catching up. I want to hear everything about how you found each other tomorrow," she adds, pointing to me before she picks up her wine and pushes open her front door.

I unlock my door then usher him inside. I'm about to step in myself when Lilah pops her head back out and mouths, *He's hot.*

"He's a friend," I whisper, but I can tell by her expression that she doesn't believe me. Unlike me, Lilah is more than happy with the friends with benefits thing.

I give her a stern look, then head inside to find Renly leaning against the wall of my entryway. "I'm sorry I didn't get to meet her back in high school."

"Her family lived in Los Angeles until they moved to Castaic. They bought that ranch that went into foreclosure. She's cool, but she's also a pain in my ass."

He laughs. "I'm glad you found such a good friend."

Happiness blooms in me. Because Lilah really is a good friend, and it's clear that Renly still knows me well enough to realize that.

"At any rate, I like her."

"Thank you for the seal of approval." I sweep my hand, ushering him into the rest of the place. It's small, only a two bedroom, one of which I use as an office. The living room is roomy, though, and the kitchen is open and flows into the space.

The back door is an actual door, not glass, but the yard it leads to is awesome. Open and grassy with a picnic table and flowers lining the fence. Lilah tells me that when her parents bought the place, there was a fence dividing the two sides, but she took it down when she moved in. She planned to put it back up again once she found a tenant, but since the tenant turned out to be me, we've left it down. It makes for some great parties.

"I've got a pair of my dad's old pajamas that I wore when I painted my bedroom. That and one of my T-shirts should do you, right?"

"Sounds good," he says, and I lead him into my bedroom. I pull out the blue-and-white striped bottoms then grab an extra-large Disney tee that I often wear to sleep.

"Minnie Mouse?"

I shrug. "You'll do her proud."

"Right," he says as I point him to the bathroom.

While he's changing, I grab a loose maxi dress and change in the closet, then toss my wet clothes into a basket and wait for Renly to emerge and give me his. He does, and then he follows me to the laundry area off the kitchen, where I start a load of cold.

I'm about to offer him the full tour when I see him rubbing his temple, one hand pressed against the wall.

"Are you okay?"

"I'm fine. Just a headache."

"Oh. I think I've got some ibuprofen. I should probably offer you that instead of the drink I was planning to suggest."

"Actually, bourbon if you have it. Believe it or not, whiskey helps."

"But when doesn't it, really?"

He grins. "We always did think alike."

I bring us both drinks and sit on the opposite end of the sofa, then shift around to get more comfortable. He pats his thighs.

I laugh, then put my bare feet in his lap, so that my back is against the arm rest. It's comfortable and easy, more so than I would have expected after so many years. But we've sat like this a hundred thousand times before, talking late into the night or watching television or just gossiping about school.

I realize that he's watching me, his eyes crinkling at the corners.

"What?"

"Don't take this the wrong way," he says, "but I didn't realize how much I missed you until I saw you."

Happiness spreads through me like warm thick syrup. "Yeah," I say. "I know exactly what you mean."

# Chapter Five

She'd been wearing sandals, and now her feet were bare in his lap. They each had a glass of bourbon, and there was a full bottle on the coffee table.

And Renly was very, very aware of the pressure of her heels on his thighs. He lifted his glass and took a sip, enjoying the burn as he swallowed. He felt the fire spread through him, and he tried to blame it all on the drink.

It wasn't just the drink.

It was seeing her again. The eagerness with which she'd flown into his arms.

It was teasing her, the water fight at the car wash, and the way his cock had stiffened when that wet tee had strained against her breasts.

It was the smell of her on the shirt he was wearing, and the pressure of her feet on his thighs. The heat seeping through the cotton PJ bottoms, then sliding into his veins, coursing through him and reminding him of those last few months before he'd left Castaic. The months when all he'd been able to think about was Abby, even though he'd never worked up the nerve to tell her. How could he? They'd been friends. *Friends.* And no way was he going to screw that up by telling her he'd been jerking off every night to the fantasy that she'd sneak over and into his room the way they'd used to in sixth grade.

He hadn't told her then, and he wasn't going to tell her now, even though he longed to pull her down on the couch, then silence her gasp of surprise with a hard, punishing kiss, wild and deep enough to erase his fantasies. Or fulfill them.

"Renly."

Because why the hell would he need them if he had reality?

"*Renly!*"

He shook himself, turning to her and praying he hadn't said any of that aloud. "Sorry? What?"

"I said that tickles."

He realized he'd been stroking the ball of her foot with the pad of his thumb. "Oh. Sorry."

"No, it's okay. It felt nice. At least until it started to tickle." She cleared her throat, and her cheeks turned a little pink, and he had the feeling that she was bullshitting. That it didn't tickle at all, and she just wanted him to stop stroking her skin.

And that was a damn shame.

He cleared his throat and shifted on the sofa, using the movement as an excuse to pull his hands away. "So tell me about these calls," he said because that seemed like the safest possible topic.

"It's probably just paranoia," she said. "I told you on the street. Heavy breathing. Hangups. A real pain."

"Any texts?"

She shook her head.

"Voicemails?"

"Yes, but just silence. The breathing's only when I answer, but I don't answer my cell. Just the office phone. It doesn't have caller ID. And during business hours, Marge takes the calls at the front desk."

"Any bad dates recently?"

She made a snorting noise. "Nothing but bad dates," she said. "But not very many of them. And I don't think any of the guys seem like the type."

"You never know. Tell me about them. Names, where you met them, all the details. I'll check them out."

"Yeah, well." She drew in a breath. "God, this is embarrassing."

"Dating?" He nodded sagely. "Yeah. Pathetic."

"You're so not funny. No, the details. It was, you know, one of those apps. A friend of mine designed it, so I'm in the beta program, and—"

"Your friend's name?"

"What? No, it's not him."

He stared her down until she conceded, and he wrote Cedric's name and details in his phone to follow up on tomorrow. "And the actual dates? Or were they just hookups?"

"No. No, no." She shook her head. "I'll forward all the information

I have later," she promised. "It's not like you're going to track them down tonight. But they were *not* hookups."

"Right," he said, a bit alarmed by her tone. "Sorry for misunderstanding."

"Oh, hell," she said, then shifted on the sofa and pulled her knees up, which had the unfortunate side-effect of removing her feet from his lap.

He turned so he was looking at her more directly. "Abby, what's going on?"

"I don't do hookups," she said. "I mean, I know that makes me some sort of prehistoric weirdo, but it's not my thing. I'm not interested in hookups or friends-with-benefits or any of that. I want—" She shook her head. "Never mind. Getting off topic." She drew in a breath. "The point of the app is to let folks have it both ways. *Tribe Find.* You can search for romance or hookups or just friends."

"And you were looking for friends?"

She lowered her eyes, her neck and ears turning pink as she said, "Romance. But it didn't work out. Not even a smidgeon of a spark. I don't know…"

"What?" He was genuinely interested. He wanted inside her head. He was fascinated by what she wanted and what made her tick.

"I just—I'd had such shit luck in the real world, I guess I hoped that filling out a profile would help. But it didn't help at all."

"The real world. Who?"

"It's—there was this guy named Travis who worked with me. And we started going to dinner sometimes, and then we started sleeping together."

With every word, Renly felt a tightening in his gut, and he realized that he really, really didn't like this Travis guy. "Did he hurt you?"

"No, nothing like that."

"I don't mean physically."

A smile flickered on her lips, and her voice was softer when she said, "No. Thanks, though. No, it wasn't that he hurt me. I guess it was that we didn't understand each other. We started hanging out together, then sleeping together. And I thought it was going somewhere, and he thought it was friends with benefits. But it got to where we couldn't even go to a movie without ending up in bed."

"And that was bad?"

She lifted her hands. "I wanted a relationship—something real, you know. He just wanted fun. I finally told him that we had to stop."

"He was okay with that?"

Something that might have been pain flashed over her face, but she nodded. "Eventually, yeah. But it was hard getting back on track. I shouldn't have ever slept with him in the first place."

"Do you think he—"

"No. Absolutely not."

She was adamant, but Renly wasn't convinced. He nodded, but at the same time he made a mental note to check this Travis guy out.

"How about you?"

He didn't have to ask what she meant. Of all the friends he'd ever had, it was always Abby he understood perfectly. This time, though, he wasn't sure he wanted to answer. But he did, because she deserved to hear the truth, just like she'd told him the truth. "I guess I'm the opposite. I'm not a big fan of relationships. Sex I like, though. So the concept of friends with benefits suits me just fine."

"Oh. Why?"

*That* was not a subject he was getting into now, so he just shook his head and asked, "You really didn't know I was in town?"

"Not a clue. I already told you that. And why are you changing the subject?"

He exhaled, then decided he'd rather she hear it from him. "You know I've been working in Hollywood. Well, I've been dating there, too. Francesca Muratti and Marissa McQuire. A few others, but those were the ones that landed my picture all over social media."

She shook her head. "I've never really paid much attention to celebrity gossip, but I know the names. They're both huge. You're saying that you dated both of them."

"More like fuck-buddies," he said. "I'm not really the relationship type." It was who he was—who he always had been, at least since high school. Before that, he'd been sure he'd marry Abby and they'd move to Hawaii. He'd never been to Hawaii, but it seemed exotic, and at eleven the idea of marriage had seemed exotic enough that Hawaii made sense.

Now he knew how foolish he'd been. Getting serious with Abby would have been a mistake. Hell, they wouldn't even be here now, having this conversation, because it would have invariably fallen apart, and then they would have lost everything, this perfect, easy friendship most of all.

"Why not?" she asked, and it took him a second to realize that she was asking why he didn't do relationships.

"It's just—I don't think it ever works out the way people think it will."

"Wow. Well, that just makes me sad. Why?"

He lifted his hands, then let them fall. Then flat-out changed the subject, easing back to their childhood. At first, he thought she was going to protest. But soon enough they were both on their third glass of whiskey and laughing their asses off remembering the time they'd tried to build a treehouse. "The look on your face when you fell though that flooring."

"Hey, I could have killed myself."

"Nah," she said with a grin. "You're indestructible. That's why you make such a great military guy. And Stark Security guy. What?" she added with a frown, apparently noticing something in his expression.

He forced a smile. "Nothing. I'm just thinking you make a good point. I wasn't built for either architecture or constuction. Construction," he said, realizing he'd had just enough whiskey to be pleasantly buzzed.

"You should stay here," she said. "It's silly to take an Uber home only to come back to the area tomorrow to get your bike. Plus, this couch is super comfy."

He patted the cushion, hoping she couldn't tell the way that her suggestion that he stay had perked up every cell in his body, only to have them sagging in disappointment when she made it clear that he'd be camping on the couch.

"I don't know," he began.

"Oh, come on. It's getting late, but I don't want to stop talking. Do you?"

"No," he said honestly. Right then, he felt like he could talk to her forever. More, that he wanted to. "Do you remember the time we decided to run away?"

"Are you kidding? Of course. Third grade and we had different teachers. It was horrible."

"And you had a friend who was homeschooled, and when our parents said no way, we decided to homeschool ourselves."

"It seemed reasonable at the time," she said, and he chuckled with the memory.

"We each took an encyclopedia, water, and potato chips," he said. "I had X-Y-Z."

"Because it was the thinnest and you were lame," she said, and he really did laugh.

"Not lame. Just lazy. Not like you. I had to talk you out of taking three because they were heavy. You said we'd sneak back for others after we read each one, and by the time we came home, we'd know everything there was to know."

"It was a good plan," she said. "Just missing some key pieces of, um—"

"Reality?"

"That about covers it," she admitted.

They shared a smile, and he felt so damn settled. It was a good feeling, and terrifying too, because he knew so well that it could all evaporate in an instant. It had with his parents, after all. His mom going deaf. His father packing up and leaving. Being dragged to Houston when he wanted to stay firmly at home. And in Iraq as well. Close friends, gone in an instant. His own life changed in the blink of an eye.

"Hey?" Her gentle voice pulled him from his dark thoughts. "Did I lose you?"

"I miss those days," he said honestly.

"Me too." She took another sip of her drink. "I'm a little tipsy, or I probably wouldn't say this, even though I'm sure you already know."

"Yeah? What?"

"I had a total crush on you freshman year."

"No way."

She nodded firmly. "Oh, yes. But you were so popular, and I thought you'd forgotten I existed."

Her words were like a knife to his heart.

"God no. I kept—I was afraid to hang out with you."

"What? Why?"

He drew a breath. "Because I couldn't stop thinking of you. I had this fantasy that you'd knock on my window one night, and I'd let you in, and—"

He shook his head, cutting off the words. "But we'd never been like that—we were friends—and I thought if you saw it in my eyes, I'd lose you. The same way I lost my dad. He didn't even try to work it out with my mom. It just got hard and he couldn't deal and he left."

"You thought that would happen to us?"

"I wanted you as a friend more than I wanted you in bed—hell, back then I didn't even know what that would be like. Not really. But I imagined it in living color."

"Yeah?" She scooted closer, her knees pulled up inside that pale pink dress. "So, um, how was I?"

He swallowed, trying not to look at the way her nipples were tight against the thin material. Or the way her pulse was beating in her neck. He needed to stop this. Needed to back it down, because this conversation had taken a dangerous—enticing—left turn. Keep going, and he'd regret it. He knew it.

And yet somehow he couldn't quite veer off the path. "You were amazing," he whispered. "And you tasted like strawberries."

"It's the lip balm," she said. "I still use it."

Their eyes met, and dear God he was hard.

"Do you want to taste? See if it's like it was in your fantasy?" She bit her lower lip. "I've never been anyone's fantasy before."

"I find that very hard to believe." He didn't mention her potential stalker. He should—it would kill the mood, and this was a mood that really should be killed. But damn him all to hell, he didn't say a single thing.

"Whiskey and strawberries," she said, then leaned forward, her hands on his thighs. She glanced down, and he heard her sharp intake of breath, then saw the heat in her eyes when she looked back up. "You do want," she said as she slid her hand higher until her fingertips barely brushed his cock under the thin cotton of those damned pajama bottoms.

"Abby, what are you doing?"

"Are you honestly telling me you haven't figured that out yet?"

He had to laugh. "I have a clue, believe me. Oh, shit—" He swallowed hard as her hand closed over his cock. "Abby…"

He saw a flash of either hurt or frustration as she started to pull away. He acted without thinking, closing his hand over hers, keeping her hand on his cock as he met her eyes. "What happened to you don't do casual sex?"

"I—Don't you want to know what we missed out on? Aren't you curious?"

*Hell yes he was.*

"I'm not—Abby, I'm so glad we found each other again, and believe me, I am not saying no."

Her mouth quirked, and she cupped her hand more firmly around him. "No, you're definitely not."

"I'm not looking for a relationship. And you don't do casual sex. So what exactly are you looking for here?"

"Just tonight," she said. "Because I missed you, and I trust you."

*Trust.* What woman he'd ever been with had used that as a come-on? But damned if those simple words hadn't pushed him over the edge.

She was right—they both deserved this. To know what they might have had if he'd stayed. If he hadn't acted like an ass and dated every other girl except the one who'd stolen his heart back when he was in diapers.

"All right," he said, pushing her hand off his cock. "But we're going to take this slow."

# Chapter Six

"Slow," I repeat. "Yeah, I think I like that."

"And we do this my way." His hand closes over mine, and he moves me gently but firmly off his cock.

"That doesn't seem fair," I say.

"I like being in charge," he says, easing me back until I'm once again leaning against the arm of the sofa. My feet are tucked under me, and he tells me to straighten them. "On my legs again," he says. "Just as we were."

"What—"

"Abby. Just do it."

I swallow a protest, mostly because I'm curious, and slip my bare feet back onto his thighs.

"Do you want to know what I was thinking earlier? My fantasy of how the evening could go? What I wanted to do, but didn't have the fucking balls? Not like you did, starting this whole thing up. Is that what you want, Abby? Do you want to know what I was thinking earlier? Is that really where you want me to take you?"

There's heat and harshness in his voice, and I nod. Right then, I want nothing more than to see into his fantasies. To know if his were as wild and wicked as mine have been. How he wanted me. What he would do to me. Because every kiss or stroke or touch just goes that much further to validate the intense passion building inside me, not to mention my own boldness.

"Yes," I say. "But you have to remember something when you do."

He turns to meet my eyes.

"Just remember that I'm the one who had the balls to start this."

His mouth twitches. "And for that, I think we're both very, very grateful."

His hand strokes my foot as he speaks. "We were talking like this earlier," he says softly. "And it wasn't even that long ago, but I have to struggle to remember what we were saying. Because that wasn't the only conversation in my head. There was another one. My voice telling me to let go. To touch you the way I wanted to."

"How did you want to?" My words are a whisper, and my whole body tingles.

"Gently," he says, running his fingertip along the side of my foot. "An exploration," he continues, slowly stroking my ankle, then my calf, then cupping me behind my knee. "A game to see when you would tell me to stop."

"I wouldn't have," I say, then draw in air as he shifts on the couch, too, coming closer to me and forcing me to bend one knee up so that the ball of my foot is pressed against his cock, hard beneath my sole. He bends at the waist, one hand on that foot increasing the pressure as he meets my eyes, and the other hand stroking north on my other leg.

He's reached the hem, and his fingertip slips under the loose cotton of the maxi dress, brushing my thigh just above my knee.

I whimper, and I see a gleam that looks like victory spark in his eye. "What will I find if I keep going north?" he asks. "Cotton panties? Silk? Or are you completely bare under that dress? I know you're not wearing a bra. I've been mesmerized by your breasts all night."

"Renly..."

My voice sounds breathy and unfamiliar.

"I'm betting nothing," he says, and I close my eyes, not willing to acknowledge out loud that he's right. Even more, not willing to admit—even to myself—that it was the fantasy of a moment like this that had me forgoing panties in the first place. "Should I keep going? Should I tease your pussy? See if you're wet? Slide my fingers inside you and watch your face as you try not to grind against me?"

I make a low noise in my throat, a noise of longing. Of desperation.

"Or should I stop here and kiss your mouth? Tasting and taking? Fucking your mouth with my tongue until you're weak and limp and begging for more?"

My head is spinning. I've gotten myself off to so many fantasies of Renly's touch, of his kisses. But never have I imagined him saying these things, raw and wild and so very appealing. I want it all, and while part of me hates that he's seeing me so needy and desperate, a bigger part of me is turned on by the fact that it's him who's made me this way—and that, of course, he knows it.

"Tell me," he says, sliding off the couch and kneeling in front of me. He spreads my legs, and though the dress is still draped to my knees, I feel exposed. And, so help me, it feels wonderful.

His hands ease up my thighs beneath the dress. I whimper, lost in the sensations that are ricocheting through me now. Slowly, his fingers rise, higher and higher as he gently parts my legs. My breath trembles, and I'm burning with the anticipation of his touch. His thumbs are *right there*, brushing that soft, sensitive skin.

"Tell me," he repeats. "Should I touch you or kiss you?"

I suck in a breath, my whole body trembling. "Couldn't you please do both?"

He laughs. "God, I love you."

I tense, those words crashing over me. He doesn't react at all, and I realize he doesn't know what he said. But he *did* say it. And damned if I don't love him too. Not that I have the chance to say so, though, because he's doing exactly what I asked. His mouth is hot on mine, his thumbs teasing my core. I spread my legs wider as his fingers thrust inside me, the kiss just as wild and hot, our tongues doing battle as if this kiss alone could take us both over the edge.

I moan in protest as he breaks the kiss, then gasp when he lifts my ass to free the dress. "Take it off," he demands, though he doesn't leave it to me. He's back on the couch, his hands now on the material, pulling it up over my head and leaving me completely naked.

"Now close your eyes and put your arms on the back of the couch. And baby, spread your legs for me."

I hesitate, the thought of being so exposed making me both excited and nervous. Mostly excited, though, and my nipples tighten and my core throbs as I do as he asked, feeling all the more vulnerable because my eyes are closed.

I feel his hands on my thighs just above my knees. He moves them higher until his thumbs are brushing the junction of my thighs. I tremble and bite my lower lip. I'm so wet—so turned on—and he can see everything. And damned if that doesn't make me even more turned on. This vulnerability. This exposure.

With wicked slowness, he kisses his way up my inner thigh. I bite my lip, forcing myself to stay still. Then he lifts his mouth away long enough to blow a stream of air right on my clit. I arch back, clutching the back of the sofa, then relax—even whimper—when he stops.

"Tell me," he says.

"More," I whisper. "Please, I want more. Renly, I want you."

"Patience, baby," he whispers, brushing a kiss over my lips, then letting his lips roam lower and lower until his tongue flicks lightly over my clit. I suck in air, almost exploding right then, but he's barely even started. Now his mouth closes over my sex, and he sucks and teases as I try to squirm, but his hands are firmly on my thighs now, holding me in place.

I know it's breaking the rules, but I don't care. I move my hands, then twine my fingers in his hair. I hold tight, practically forcing him to stay in place. To suck my clit and fuck me with his tongue. I want more—oh, God, I'm greedy—but first I have to let go of some of this pressure.

First, I have to explode.

As if the thought is a touch, my body breaks apart. I yank on his hair, and it's probably a miracle I don't pull out chunks as I buck and writhe against him, this man I've loved forever, this friend I never really knew before. Not like this. Not as a man who fits me so damn perfectly.

"Oh, God," I say when I can speak again. "Renly, my God."

He lifts his head, then slides up my body before kissing me, giving me a taste of my own passion. "I'm very glad you liked it."

An almost hysterical laugh escapes me. "*Like* has never before been such an understatement."

"I'm very glad to hear it. But baby, you know we're not done." He kisses me gently then slides his lips over my cheek to my ear to whisper, "I still haven't fucked you, and believe me, that is very much on tonight's agenda."

I swallow and nod, then take his hand when he stands and reaches out for me. He leads me to the bedroom, then nods for me to stretch out. I do, then watch eagerly as he strips out of my shirt and PJ bottoms, freeing his cock. He's already grabbed a condom from the wallet he'd left on the coffee table, and I reach up to tease my own nipples as he sheaths himself.

"Christ, that's hot," he says.

"You like it?"

"I do." He gets onto the bed, sitting next to me and idly stroking his fingertips over my bare skin. "Touch yourself more," he says. "Show me what you did when we were kids. When you were in bed late at night, fantasizing that I'd climbed through your window."

"Renly…" My cheeks are burning.

"Here," he says, "I'll help you." He puts his hand over mine, then together we lightly tease my nipple before he guides my fingers down over my abdomen, then around my navel until we reach my pussy. I'm waxed, and he slides my fingertips over smooth skin before landing on my slick, sensitive clit.

"Inside," he says, his own fingers teasing my clit as he waits for me to comply. "Tell me the truth," he continues. "You'd fingerfuck yourself, wouldn't you? And you'd pretend it was me."

"Yes." It's the truth, but I'm so turned on I would have lied even if it wasn't.

"Show me."

I don't hesitate—all hesitation and embarrassment have been washed away by a wild, sensual greed. I do as he says, thrusting three fingers inside myself as my hips move in time with my own demands. My eyes are closed, but I feel the way his hand tenses as he cups my mound. The way his breathing has become more ragged.

And then, finally, he growls, "Enough."

I open my eyes, surprised, only to lose myself in a hard, punishing kiss as he moves on top of me. "I don't want to take it slow," he says.

"No," I say, wanting him to just take, and to do it hard. "Not slow."

I see heat flare in his eyes before he reaches between our bodies to adjust himself. And then, in one long, deep thrust, he spreads me wide and buries himself inside me.

I close my eyes, arching back as he pounds into me, deep and hard, teasing all my sensitive spots with the girth of him filling me and his fingers on my clit. Deeper and deeper, and when he tells me to open my eyes, I do, and I look into his as we move in rhythm together until finally—finally—I explode around him, my body clenching tightly to his cock.

He arches up, cries out, then collapses beside me. For a moment, he is completely motionless. Then he rolls over and kisses me, his fingers casually playing with my nipple as if he owns me. Which, of course, he does.

"That," he says. "That was *my* fantasy."

I sigh happily. "Yeah," I say. "Me, too."

# Chapter Seven

Renly stood in Abby's bathroom, his hands pressed to the Formica countertop, his eyes staring straight into his own in the mirror. *Christ, last night was incredible. Making love, but also simply holding her in his arms and talking as they drifted off to sleep.*

*Yeah, absolutely wonderful.*

And a mistake. A wonderful, terrible mistake.

He drew a deep breath, the weight of regret drowning out the shouts of joy that were ricocheting inside of him. This was on him. He should've said no.

She'd flat-out told him that she wasn't a casual sex kind of girl. They'd talked about it. She'd opened up to him in a way they hadn't done since they were kids, when no topic was too dicey.

So what that she'd said yes?

So what that she'd made the first move and sworn to him it was okay?

Deep down, it wasn't what she wanted, and he knew that. That was the whole point of their talk last night. The whole reason why she'd quit dating that guy Travis. The whole reason why she'd gotten on that app. To try to find someone permanent. Something real.

It was old-fashioned and sweet and a little quaint, and he imagined that there were a lot of people in the world who thought that she was a fool for wanting that integrity. He wasn't one of those people. He really wasn't.

And yet he'd still pulled her close. He'd still buried himself inside her in a goddamned wave of passion. He'd still done everything wrong, and damned if it hadn't felt so very right.

"You're an idiot. You know that, right?" His reflection just stared back at him, unwilling to share its secrets or share the blame.

He turned on the tap and splashed cold water on his face. Then he grabbed the towel, dried off, and opened the bathroom door. She was sitting on the edge of the bed in the Minnie Mouse shirt looking at him. He felt the weight of accusation in her eyes, but when he looked close he didn't actually see it. It was all in his imagination.

"It's okay, you know."

He smiled, shaking his head in mock exasperation. "You're reading my mind."

Her smile spread into a delighted grin, and the trill of her laughter eased his guilt. "It's what I'm good at, remember? We always knew what each other was thinking."

He nodded and returned to sit beside her on the bed. She scooted over so that her back was against the headboard, and he shifted so that he was facing her.

"Are we okay?"

Once again, he wanted to laugh. "Under the circumstances, I think I should be the one asking you that."

"We're fine," she said, reaching for his hand. "We're really, really fine."

"Listen," he began, then cleared his throat. "I, um, I just want to be clear. The truth is I would happily have a repeat performance of last night, but I know you don't want that."

He paused to watch her face, but her expression was entirely unreadable. The only clue as to what was going on inside her head was the way her eyes widened just slightly. But he didn't know how to read that, so he just pressed on. "I won't ask. I won't push. I don't want..."

"What?"

"I don't want to toss away what I think we got back by letting sex get in the way. I know this was a one-off. I know it, and I'm cool with that. I suppose I should probably regret sleeping with you at all," he said. "But I don't. We found each other again, and we both had a good time, but it was a one-off. No friends with benefits, right? But I still really want to keep the friend part, and I want to make sure that we're on the same page."

Her face lit with her smile. "You really are the last gentleman standing," she said as she took his hand. "And I really do have great taste in friends."

He studied her face. "So we're good? You don't feel weird about the whole thing?"

"I don't. I really don't. And I'm so grateful for everything that you're saying. Last night, it felt... It felt like a great reunion, and it felt like taking care of old business. And all of that is good. Because it also felt like a start."

"And you don't want to keep on...?"

"I—" She shook her head, then cleared her throat. "I told you. I'm not interested in a friends-with-benefits thing. Flings aren't my style." She leaned forward and took his hands. "But if I was that girl, I would totally be into it with you, at least so long as it didn't screw up our friendship. Because I can't tell you how glad I am to have you back."

"Friends forever," he said, then extended his elbow in the bizarre version of a handshake they'd come up with in fifth grade. A laugh bubbled out of her, and she bumped her elbow with his.

"Forever," she said.

He nodded, and though he was glad about the outcome, he couldn't deny the little voice in his head that told him he was closing the door on something extraordinarily special.

# Chapter Eight

"So how'd it go?"

Renly's been gone for about an hour; he left after giving me strict orders to lock the place up and not open the door to strangers. I've been buzzing through my apartment since, burning off energy by cleaning. He's gone to get his bike and run some errands, but he's coming back in a few hours to escort me to the office and check it out before my afternoon meeting with Darrin. I'm not worried—not really—but I'd feel pretty stupid if some scary stalker was hiding under my desk.

Marge is coming in, too, which is a plus. She does all the client billing, and often works on Saturdays. So it'll be good to have someone else in the office, if only because it looks more professional than just me and Darrin huddled behind a computer.

Right now, though, Lilah's here, and her question is forcing me to take a break and process everything that's going through my head.

"It went great," I say, which is the absolute literal truth. "We caught up. It was awesome hanging out with him again. We still really, really click." As I say the last, I feel my cheeks start to burn and I quickly look down.

Lilah, of course, misses nothing. "Oh my God," she says. "You slept with him."

"No, I—"

"Do not even," she says. "Now tell me everything."

I sigh, silently conceding the truth. "I have no idea how it happened," I admit. "We were catching up, and we'd been drinking whiskey, and we were both really chill, and then ..." I trail off with a shrug, and Lilah squeals and starts to clap.

"I'm so happy for you. This is like the best thing ever. Dating your best friend."

I shake my head. "No. It was a one-time thing."

She tilts her head to the side. "You? A one-time thing? This does not sound like the friend I have known and loved since sophomore year."

I shrug. "I wanted him," I admit. "And we talked about it. It was all very mature and open. I told him that I don't do friends with benefits, and he told me that he wasn't interested in getting serious, and—"

"And yet you ended up in bed together?"

Once again, I shrug. "He's my old crush. What can I say? I broke my rule. But just for the one time. We talked about it afterwards. It's very mature," I repeat. "We're still friends. We're *just* friends. We're only going to be friends."

"And you're okay with that?"

I force myself not to shrug this time. Instead I lift my chin, straighten my back, and very firmly say, "Yes. I respect that he doesn't want a relationship. He's not interested in settling down."

"I'm not surprised. He's dated like every A-list actress in the city."

"He told me," I say. "All part of the same conversation. And like I said, we're not sleeping together again. We're just friends. He can sleep with whoever he wants to, celebrity or not."

At the same time, I have to admit to myself that I'm glad he's not working in Hollywood anymore. He seemed so sad when he told me that he wasn't interested in a relationship because they just don't work. He had that *I'm being practical* tone, but there was something else beneath it.

"Where did you go?" Lilah asks.

I shake my head. "Just thinking. He told me that he's not a relationship guy, and I'm thinking it has to do with his parents."

"Yeah?" She heads to my fridge and pulls out a watermelon-flavored sparkling water. She holds it up. "Want one?"

"No, but thanks so much for offering."

She makes a face. "Hey. We share the house. What's mine is yours and what's yours is mine."

"This is why I love you. We should just put a door between our units."

She laughs. "From your bedroom to my living room. Think of all the entertainment value that would bring to me." She pops the top on her drink and comes back to sit on the couch next to me. "So what about his family?"

"I think the issues with his parents started when his mom lost her hearing, but I'm guessing there were problems before, too. She had some sort of autoimmune disorder, and it happened really, really fast. Apparently it's super rare, and there's really not anything they can do for it unless they catch it in time, and even then there aren't a lot of options."

"I'm guessing they didn't catch it in time?"

"No. Not at all."

"This was freshman year?"

"No. Junior high. And not soon after, his parents divorced. Apparently one day Mr. Cooper told her that he couldn't handle the fact that she couldn't hear anymore, and he didn't know how to process all the grief and whatnot that she was feeling, and so he just up and moved to the Northeast somewhere. I think he went to Boston. I know he ended up in New York, but I don't know the exact timing of it."

"Oh my God. What an asshole."

I nod. "Yeah. Nobody was very impressed with him. And I know that it really messed Renly up. Red, too. His brother," I add in explanation.

"He sort of went into a shell. All angry and alone. Red kind of acted out against his dad. They were both pissed that he was such a jerk to their mom. It was tough. And I remember their mom was trying to deal with it, going to doctors trying to get her hearing back, but that didn't work, so she had teachers come over to try and help her cope and teach her and the boys how to lip read and learn sign language and all that stuff."

I get up and go get my own soda. I come back, pop the top, and take a long swallow. "Anyway, I guess they have family in Texas, because that summer after freshman year, she ended up packing up the boys and moving to Houston."

I meet Lilah's eyes. "That's really all there is. I don't know what happened to them once they got down there, but I do know that it was a really nasty divorce. It must have been horrible for them."

My parents are as thick as thieves, and they always have been. They were high school sweethearts, and now they're still just as gooey as they probably were back then. I would say it's disgusting if it weren't so adorable.

"I think it messed him up," I tell Lilah. "I think he doesn't trust relationships. His parents always seemed so close. And then suddenly this one horrible thing happens, and his dad completely lost his shit. And then their whole world fell apart."

"So he fucks around because his parents got divorced?"

I pull my feet up onto the couch and sigh. "I don't know. I'm not a shrink. All I know is that he says he's not interested in a relationship, and I believe him. And it's not like it's even something that is on my mind. I mean, I'm just happy he's back in my life."

"But you slept with him."

"I know. It was stupid. But it was awesome too."

Lilah leans back and laughs. "I am so glad to hear that."

"But we're not doing it again. He was my best friend. You have to get that. I mean, we're super close now, but he and I were closer than you and I ever were in high school. I mean, we used to actually take baths together when we were little kids."

"I cannot even begin to tell you how glad I am that we do not take baths together."

"Ha ha."

"I get it," she says, "I really do. You're happy he's back in your life, you don't want anything to screw that up, and you're just a little bit afraid that sleeping with him last night is going to do that."

"Yes. Exactly."

"Have you talked to him about it?"

"Yes. We both agree that it's all good, it's in the past, and we're just friends."

"Then you don't have any problem."

"Nope," I say. "No problem at all."

No problem except for the fact that I really do want to do it all over again, and I hate myself for it because that would be breaking my own rules. Not to mention risking a friendship, and all because the boy I once lusted for is back in my life again.

\* \* \* \*

Renly and I get to the office at one and find Darrin already in the waiting room for our two o'clock appointment. Marge is there, too, and she looks a little harried. I don't blame her; she's had to babysit Darrin for an hour.

I shoot her an apologetic glance and force myself to smile, even though I really want to crawl to my office and have a few moments alone. Why the hell don't people come at an appointed time? Don't they realize that I have things to do before I'm ready for them?

"Have a good day," Renly says, and I can hear the sympathy in his tone, though I'm sure Darrin won't pick up on it. "Call me if Marge needs to leave," he says, adding her to the conversation. "Otherwise, I'll be back at five."

"Sounds good," I say. "See you then."

Renly leaves, and I feel a pang of regret as the door shuts behind him. Then I force myself to aim a business-appropriate smile at Darrin. "I'm so glad you're here. Give me just a little bit to get set up and I'll bring you in so we can run through the demo."

He'd been pushing out of his chair as I spoke, and now he settles back down again, looking a little bit frustrated. Well, too bad for him. I'm a little bit frustrated, too. I hurry to my office and fire up my computer. As I'm tapping my desk, waiting for the login screen to show up, Eric slides into my doorway, making me jump.

"I didn't know you were coming in today."

He shrugs. "Catchup." He cocks his head vaguely in the direction of the front office, his thick blond hair gleaming in the lighting. "I saw you had company."

I roll my eyes. "He's not supposed to be here for another hour. I have things to tweak before I run him through the demo."

Eric shrugs. "He's new at Greystone-Branch. He's eager to prove his worth."

I nod. I know he's right.

"Do you want me to go entertain him?"

"Thanks, but poor Marge is on it. What are you doing here on the weekend?"

"Trying to catch up on all the projects. I know Nikki did me a favor bringing me back, and I don't want to let her down."

Eric was hired about the same time that I was, when Nikki first decided she needed to bring on a team to help her with her business. We'd gotten along great, but then Eric had been offered a sweet job in New York. Nikki and I had both been surprised when he left, because he'd been doing so well at her company, and there was so much room for growth. But Eric had stars in his eyes, and they tossed a lot of money at him and offered him all sorts of perks. From what he said, though, it didn't fit his personality. He was a cog in the machine, and he hated it.

He'd come back, and Nikki eventually offered him his old job again. Now I'm technically his boss, which to Eric's credit, hasn't seemed to weird him out at all. That's one thing I always liked about him. He's about the work more than the position.

He takes a step forward and peers at my computer. "You still haven't shown me the platform."

"You can sit in on the meeting if you want to. I'd love to have your thoughts on any tweaks you might want made."

"I can if you want me to." He reaches out and brushes my shoulder. Immediately, I tense, then just as quickly relax. I hope he didn't notice. I realized in the moment that he was brushing a leaf from the hallway ficus off my shoulder, and I turn my attention back to my computer to hide my embarrassment.

He clears his throat. "All right, I'm going to go finish up. Give a shout if you want me to join the meeting."

"Will do, thanks."

I run through the platform and my various notes and make sure I've got my ducks in order, then buzz Marge to bring him to the conference room. I take my laptop and meet them there. "Sorry I got here so early," he says. "I wasn't sure about the traffic."

"Not a problem at all," I say, my voice completely cheerful and chirpy now that I'm feeling in control of the situation. I hook my laptop into the system and project onto the dropdown screen.

To Darrin's credit, he's both sharp and invested. He's got a very studious manner about him, and after almost every comment, he asks me what I think or praises my work. Twice he tells me how talented I am, and I can't deny that makes me happy. When we finally wrap, I know that we have a satisfied client.

"Bijan is going to be thrilled," Darrin says. "I'll tell him things are going along nicely."

"We should be able to roll it out in the next ten days," I tell him.

"That's terrific. Why don't I plan to come back in a few days from now for final tweaks and review?"

"Perfect," I say. "We can get Bijan and the rest of the gang involved through a video call."

He tells me that sounds like a good plan, then stands, his hand extended for me to shake. I do, a little unnerved by the sticky dampness of his skin. I've never been a fan of handshaking, and I resist the urge to wipe my palm on my slacks once he breaks contact. I walk him out, then go back to my office and spend a couple more hours implementing the changes that we discussed. I'm about to leave again when my phone rings. I assume it's Renly since Marge let the call through, and I answer it.

Immediately, I regret it. It's my mouth breather. I listen, feeling sick to my stomach as he just sits and breathes heavily on the other end of the phone. "Pervert," I say, then slam the phone down before buzzing Marge and asking why she put him through.

"No calls came for you," she tells me. "He must have your direct line."

I already know that, of course, since I've been getting the calls for days. But hope springs eternal and all that. I make a mental note to ask Nikki about changing my direct line number.

It wouldn't be that inconvenient. After all, I don't give out the direct dial to that many people. We'll inconvenience a few clients, but if it stops this creep, I can live with that.

I stand up, feeling squidgy, and the phone rings again. I consider just ignoring it, but instead I grab it up, and yell, "Would you stop it already?"

"I'm sorry, what?"

I cringe. "Darrin. I'm so sorry. I'm getting prank calls at work. I didn't mean to yell at you."

"Oh. Wow. I'm so sorry. Are you okay?"

"Yes, it's just some asshole calling and breathing. Stupid little—" I stop before I curse in front of a client. "Um, is there something you need?"

"I was just going to ask if you wanted to grab a late lunch. I went to the promenade and did some shopping, and I'm about to head back home, but I thought if you were hungry we could talk more about the rollout."

"Oh. You know, normally I'd love to. But I already have plans."

"Sure. Just a thought. No problem."

"Maybe a rain check?" I don't really want a rain check, so I'm not sure why I'm saying that, but it seems the polite thing to do, especially since he works for our best client.

"That sounds great. And seriously, no big deal."

I hang up, and this time I gather my things and head to the front office to wait for Renly. He follows me home on his bike to make sure I arrive okay, but despite my invitation, he doesn't stay. "Summoned to the boss," he tells me. "I'm off to see Ryan."

"Oh. Sure."

"Doors locked, right? Nobody in except Lilah, not even food delivery."

I grimace but nod. Soon, we'll have to either figure out who's doing this or change the rules, because I don't intend to walk on eggshells my entire life, especially if it's just breathing.

But not yet. I'm still spooked. And I'm very glad that Renly's watching over me.

Thankfully, Lilah is home, and I invite her over just because I'm a little stir-crazy. I tell her about the call and about Darrin's offer of lunch. "I feel bad turning him down. I mean, part of the job is to wine and dine the clients."

"Yeah, but I think you did the right thing. It was probably just him thinking about work, but you never know. And the last thing you want to do is date a client. Or make a client think you'd be interested in dating." She frowns. "Unless you are. Does Nikki have rules about that?"

"I'm not," I say. Honestly, when I think about it, I haven't been attracted to too many men recently. Travis, but that was more proximity than attraction. I mean, he was cute and fun, but my pulse never raced around him.

The truth is, the only guy that's ever really done a number on me is Renly.

But he's a guy who doesn't want me. At least not the way that I want him.

# Chapter Nine

"Sorry to drag you here on the weekend," Ryan said from behind his desk at Stark Security.

Renly leaned back in the guest chair. "Are you kidding? A trip to Dubai for a covert operation? That's the kind of thing I signed up for, remember?"

Ryan laughed. "Well, can't argue with that. Liam's already over there, so he'll take you through the mission specs when you arrive. Your plane leaves first thing Wednesday morning, and I've got a little light reading for you in the meantime." He passed Renly a thick folder of material. "At least two insertions that are going to require rappelling down a skyscraper, but from what I read in your military file, that should be up your alley."

"Yes, sir," Renly said, hoping Ryan couldn't hear the lie in his voice. He pushed the chair and stood, wanting to get the hell out of there so he could catch his breath and decide what the fuck to do. "I really appreciate your faith in me. I know I'm the new guy on the block." He extended his hand to shake. But before Ryan could take it, the floor tilted, and Renly dropped his hand to steady himself on the desk, biting back a string of colorful curses.

Ryan's brow furrowed. "Are you okay?"

"Sorry. Worked out this morning, didn't eat breakfast, and stood up too fast. I'm fine."

Ryan didn't seem to notice the lie, and soon he was back at work and Renly was in the bullpen at his own desk. He pulled open a drawer, took out a prescription bottle, and tapped out a pill. He closed his eyes, cursed softly, then dry swallowed the meds.

He stayed at his desk for a few more moments, reviewing the

paperwork that Ryan had given him. The mission pushed all his buttons. Hell, it was exactly the type of assignment that had excited him about Stark Security. International operations. Excitement. Adventure.

Something real, not the bullshit of a Hollywood set, the fake stories that were interesting but provided no real fascination for him, and the equally fake women, who seemed to want nothing more than to be on his arm or in his bed.

Presumably he was more interesting than the celebrities they were used to. Too bad he didn't find them equally as interesting.

No, the only woman he'd found remotely interesting recently was Abby. And wasn't that a kicker, considering she was the one woman he really couldn't have?

He pushed back from the desk and stood, taking it slowly to make sure the world didn't tilt beneath him again. He glanced sideways at Ryan's office, knowing he should go have a talk with his boss. He waited, working up the nerve. Then he grabbed up the folder, turned around, and headed for the exit to summon a ride share because, dammit, right now was no time for him to get on the damn bike.

Hell, if he was smart he'd sell the thing before it killed him.

But he wasn't smart. He wasn't even honest. Not with himself, and not with anybody else.

He wanted to talk to Abby, but the thought of her seeing the weakness in him made his gut twist into knots. So instead he typed a different address into the app.

\* \* \* \*

"So where does a guy go to get a drink around here?" Renly said, striding into the distillery's tasting area.

Behind the counter, Red looked up, then grinned wide. His hair was a more vibrant color than Renly's, and he'd recently begun growing a beard, but other than that they looked similar enough that people used to confuse them as kids, thinking they were identical.

Abby never did, though. She always knew exactly who was who, and it had been Renly she'd bonded with, something he'd never taken for granted.

"Did we have lunch planned today?" Red asked as Renly slid onto a stool.

"Can't a guy just drop by to see his brother?"

"A guy can. I don't know what the hell you are." He poured a shot of Cooper's Slow Burn Rye, the distillery's most popular label, and passed it to Renly.

"Funny man. How's it going in here?"

"Business is good," Red said. "We've got a dozen new commercial contracts for local restaurants, and we're running a new ad campaign. Quirky and fun. I think it's really going to drive the brand up."

"I'm glad to hear it."

"I think Dad's pretty proud. You know how he is about his bars and liquor."

Renly shrugged. "Yeah. I'm sure he's very proud."

"Listen, you know you—" Red shook his head. "Never mind. It's your thing with Dad. I'll leave it between the two of you."

"Finally. My brother sees reason."

"I'm only leaving you alone because I know you're an ass."

"If I am, I guess you are, too. Twins, after all."

"But not identical. Thank God for small favors."

Renly laughed, then leaned back in his seat. "It really is good to see you, bro."

"Likewise."

"So where's Mel?" he asked, referring to Mel Swift, Red's partner in the distillery.

"Your guess is as good as mine. He's been dealing with personal shit lately. I'm cutting him a lot of slack, but pretty soon he and I are gonna have to have a talk about pulling his weight."

"Shit. I'm sorry, man."

Red waved the words away. "It'll work out. You know Mel. He got sidetracked by something, but he'll be back and focused soon. Same old, same old."

"That guy never changes," Renly said, remembering the crazy hijinks their friend from Houston regularly got in during high school. "Don't imagine he ever will."

"True that," Red said, then grinned. "Nice to have you here, bro. But you know, I think we talked more when you were working overseas in uniform. So to what do I owe the pleasure?"

"Well, I'm about to go overseas again," Renly said. "Although this time I won't be in uniform."

"No shit?"

"Yep. I'm leaving on Wednesday. Heading to Dubai."

"So I guess you're liking working for Stark? I have to say, the guy impressed the hell out of me in New York."

"Those were some unusual circumstances," Renly said. His brother had told him all about the crazy heist and the hostages that had been held in their father's bar. "I like working for him just fine," Renly said. "But he's not there full-time. Off running the world, I suppose. Ryan Hunter's my immediate boss. He knows his shit."

"Does he?" Red leaned forward, a rag in his hand as he polished the bar, not meeting Renly's eyes. Renly drew a breath. *And here we go...*

He didn't say anything. He didn't have to. He was a twin, after all, and he knew exactly what his brother was about to say.

To Red's credit, he waited a full ten seconds before speaking, long enough that Renly started to think he was wrong.

But, of course, he wasn't.

"They're okay with you going?" Red asked, his voice casual. "I mean, with your condition?"

Renly shrugged, then took a sip of his whiskey, just as casual as you please.

Red stopped polishing the oak bar. He leaned forward, his eyes narrowing as he studied Renly. "Jesus Christ. You haven't told them."

Renly closed his eyes. "Sometimes it sucks to be a twin."

"Yeah? Well, think how much worse it would be if we were identical."

"If we both looked like you? Yeah, that would be bad."

Red didn't even flinch. "You're really not going to tell them?"

"I'll tell them. But first I'm going on this mission. First I'm doing this job. Before I start throwing obstacles in my path, I want them to know that I'm qualified. I don't want anyone looking at me like I'm a goddamn invalid. They know I can do the work, they'll overlook the hitch."

Red started to speak, but Renly held up a hand. "I don't want to hear about it."

Now Red held up two hands as if pushing Renly away. "Fine, fine. It's your life. Yours to mess up, anyway."

"That it is. And I'm not messing up."

For a moment they were both quiet. Then, out of the blue, Renly said, "Did you know Abby was in town?" He wasn't quite sure why he brought it up. She didn't have anything to do with the trip. Except for the fact that she was the one reason he was hesitating about going. He'd just reconnected with her, and he was about to leave again for what could be a two-month mission. Maybe more.

He shook his head, realizing he'd missed his brother's reply. "Say again?"

"I said I had no idea she was here."

"Yeah, turns out she's Nikki's partner. In a tech firm."

"Well, what do you know, little Abigail Jones all grown up. I imagine she grew up pretty fine. She always was adorable."

"Yeah, she still is." He felt the smile tug at his lips and tried not to show it, absolutely certain that his brother would know what he was thinking, a thought that was confirmed when Red said, "Oh, fuck no."

"What?" Renly said, though he knew perfectly well what his brother was talking about.

"You didn't. Did you?"

"I am not even going to answer that."

Red dragged his fingers through his hair. "I can't believe it. All through school you're infatuated with that girl and you sleep with her *now?* Now when you're about to go away?"

"I wasn't infatuated with her."

"The hell you weren't. I was always afraid you were going to screw it up, and I think freshman year you did. You avoided that girl like the plague. And why?"

Considering they were twins, Red and Renly were far too different. His brother just didn't understand.

But Renly had known that if they got too close, they would end up breaking apart. That's exactly what happened to his parents. His dad said it was because of his mother's deafness—that he couldn't deal—and maybe that was part of it, but not all. Renly had watched them for years, and they'd been drifting apart and drifting apart and drifting apart.

The bottom line was that people didn't stay together once they got close. They were like magnets. Get too close and all they did was repel each other.

He hated the thought that he could get too complacent with Abby. That she'd never again leap into his arms with the same enthusiasm she had yesterday.

So back in high school he did the repelling first. Not that he'd understood then what he was doing. And not that he ever expected it to last.

All he knew was that he had to keep some distance if they were to keep their friendship. But then suddenly he was thrust off to a different state.

Everything had gotten so fucked up back then. And now...

Well, now he hoped it didn't get fucked up all over again.

A group of customers entered, laughing and talking, so Renly considered that his cue to leave. He waved to his brother, then pulled open the door with a sigh. He stepped outside to wait for his Uber so he could go back and get his bike. He felt steady now. Safe. But he knew it wouldn't last. The episodes were coming more regularly, and the meds weren't helping.

And wasn't that a fucked-up reality?

He was cursing his bad luck when his phone rang, and he grinned when he saw the caller ID and took the call. "Hey, guy," Renly said. "How's life in LaLa Land?"

"Chugging along," Carson said. "Am I going to see you tonight at the wrap party?"

Carson Donnelly was the most talked-about director in Hollywood, and Renly had worked on his most recent film, *Juggernaut*, staring Francesca Muratti, who, though not exactly Renly's ex, had definitely been in his bed.

"Gotta be honest," he said. "I wasn't planning on it."

"Come on, man," Carson said. "I miss working with you, and so do a lot of other folks. Come for a while, make the circuit, then we can slink away and catch up."

"For you, I may drop by. At Matthew's?" Matthew Holt was a big-shot Hollywood producer and major player in all things entertainment. He owned what Renly called a party house. A place that sometimes hosted tame parties, and sometimes hosted gatherings that were significantly racier and required a special invitation to get in. On those days, the house served as the headquarters for a sex club called Masque.

Whatever type of party was in the house, the back room was always the Masque annex, though oftentimes people in the front room didn't know the sensual option even existed. Renly wouldn't have if Francesca hadn't taken him there once. If he did go to the party tonight, that wasn't going to be a room he visited.

"Seriously," Carson said. "The crew misses you. Don't abandon us to the exotic world of international intelligence and security. Come by and share your stories."

"Fine," Renly said. He really did enjoy the people. Even Frannie had her good points, at least when she dialed down bitch mode. "I'll swing by for a few hours."

"Excellent," Carson said. "And you might want to bring a date. Frannie's already broken up with Micah—"

"That was fast."

"—and you know as well as I do that she'll latch on to you if you don't have a buffer."

"You're making me think I shouldn't come at all."

"Come on, buddy. It'll be fun."

He didn't protest again, because Carson was right. Especially if he could get Abby to go, too. She might not be a celebrity hound, but he doubted she'd been to many Hollywood parties. A few, maybe, considering she was Nikki's partner, but surely going to one of Carson Donnelly's wrap parties would be something she got a kick out of.

"Fine," he said. "I'll be there. And I'll bring a friend."

# Chapter Ten

"I'm both jealous and sad that you're going to Dubai," I tell Renly as we step into the party. It's being held in a stunning house in the Hollywood Hills with a huge entrance hall filled with people in dark suits and colorful gowns. I pause just inside to take it all in, amazed that I'm actually at an A-list Hollywood shindig celebrating the wrap of a film intended to be next year's summer blockbuster.

"It's the kind of assignment I signed on for. But," he adds, squeezing my hand, "it's only an assignment. I'll be back."

"You better. I lost my best friend once. I don't intend to lose him again. Especially since he can get me into such cool parties."

I've never been one to follow Hollywood gossip, but even I know who Matthew Holt is, the huge entertainment mogul who owns this house. And I've heard of Carson Donnelly too, the director who invited Renly and kindly suggested that he bring a date. Bonus for me.

"Do you miss it?" I ask. "Working in Hollywood, I mean."

"I haven't been gone that long," he says. "But no. Honestly, I like where I landed. It was fun in Hollywood, and it was exciting in the military. But it's nice to have the freedom that I have working at Stark Security. I have opportunities and agency here that I wouldn't have working as a SEAL."

That makes sense to me, and I'm about to say as much when my purse vibrates, signaling a text. I pull it out and check the screen, hoping it's not my stalker.

It's not. I frown, because instead it's work. Specifically, it's Darrin.

I make a face as I look up at Renly.

"Work?" I nod, and he laughs. "Well, welcome to the land of grownups."

I roll my eyes.

"Is it urgent?"

I skim the text. "He talked to his boss and has a few tweaks that he wants to work out. He's hoping that we can get together tomorrow." I groan. "I hate going into the office on Sunday."

"I'll go with you," he says. "Tell him you can carve out an hour, and then we'll go grab brunch afterwards."

"Really?"

He smiles. "What? You think I don't like brunch?"

I laugh and start to type out that answer in the text. As I do, Renly lifts his hand, signaling to someone across the room. "I'll be right back," he says. "Unless you want to come with me?"

"Who is it?"

"The director of photography on the last film I worked on. Nice guy but a little grabby." He glances at the skimpy dress that I'm wearing, a flowing skirt with a bodice held up by barely-there spaghetti straps. "Actually, why don't you stay here?"

I smirk. "Yes, sir."

He leaves, and a moment later Darrin responds to my text, agreeing to meet at ten. I'm putting my phone away when I catch a glimpse of dark hair on a medium-build man in a black suit. I do a double-take, thinking it's Darrin, then push the thought away. If he were here, surely he would have come over.

I tell myself that I'm just imagining things since Darrin's on my mind. I turn around, looking for a waiter so I can get a drink, when I find myself mere inches away from a stunning woman, tall and lithe with one of the most famous faces in the country, possibly the world. Francesca Muratti. She towers over me, courtesy of stilettos so high it's amazing that she can walk without falling. She smiles, as friendly as a neighborhood Girl Scout, and extends her hand to me.

I take it without thinking.

"So you're the flavor of the month," she says.

"Pardon me?"

Her smile widens, showing teeth. "Renly's newest toy."

"I'm not a toy."

"Then you clearly don't know Renly."

"Yes," I say. "I do."

She takes a step back. Her head tilts as she studies me. "You definitely have moxie."

"What is your problem? You don't know me. You just decide to come over and rag on me about the man I came to this party with?"

"Are you dating him?"

"That is none of your business." This conversation is beyond surreal.

She cocks her head. "Just remember—I had him first."

"Congratulations?"

She makes a snorting noise. But I think I see something that looks like respect in her eyes.

For a moment we simply stare at each other, and it's starting to get awkward when she says, "Has he taken you to Masque yet?"

I say a silent thank you to Nikki that I know what Masque even is. We went out drinking one night after work and she told me about how Damien surprised her by taking her to the private, underground sex club.

That was the night we shifted from being coworkers to outright friends.

I, of course, have never been to Masque. But the pieces fall into place now. As we walked in, I heard someone mention that they were on their way to the club. But they hadn't left by the front door. Instead, they'd headed toward the back of the house.

I've heard other rumors, too, bits and pieces at various parties I've been to over the years. And from what I understand, sometimes Masque takes up this entire house, but sometimes it's limited to a section in the back, like an old speakeasy where you have to know the proper password.

I don't know the proper password. I don't, however, intend to admit that to Francesca. I'm sparring with the most famous movie star in the world. I want to win. I don't care about playing fair.

Which is why I lift my chin and say, "Of course. In fact, we're heading back there and going tonight."

For a moment, she doesn't react at all, and I do a series of leaps and backflips in my mind, celebrating my awesome score. Then she takes a step forward, her brow furrowing, and I am absolutely certain that she's going to ask me for details, and my bullshit is going to be called, and my victory is going to fizzle.

But then Renly walks up. My knight in shining armor. "Francesca?"

She smiles at him, that famous smile I've seen on so many posters.

"Is there a problem?"

"None at all. Your friend was just telling me that you two are going to Masque this evening."

Renly looks at me, and I try to look completely nonchalant. Then he slides his hand along my back and, very slowly, says, "Yes. In fact, we're heading there right now."

# Chapter Eleven

"Masque," he said, once Frannie was gone. He was trying to act casual, though the idea of having Abby with him in the club turned him on more than he liked to admit. "Do you even know what that is?"

"Sure," she said.

He narrowed his eyes. "Really?"

"Okay, I have a general sense. Damien took Nikki there once. After three drinks she gave me the scoop."

"Interesting."

She bit her lower lip. "I probably shouldn't have spilled that about your boss."

He laughed. "That's okay. I have a feeling Damien Stark can handle people knowing that he went to a sex club with his wife."

"You've been there," she said, and he thought he heard an accusation in her voice.

"I have."

He watched her throat move when she swallowed, wishing he could read her mind. He wanted her back there. Not for the hardcore stuff—that didn't seem like Abby, though he wouldn't turn down the chance to find out. No, he had a very specific fantasy.

He wanted her on one of the sofas in the main room. He wanted to open his fly and settle her on his lap. He wanted her skirt splayed out over them as she rose and fell, fucking him while anyone in the room who wanted to watched.

He wanted it because he wanted her. Wanted to claim her. To own her. Maybe not forever—*definitely not forever*—but for now. For tonight. For this weekend.

*Maybe forever...*

He pushed aside the voice in his head. That voice that told him that would be a good thing. That he deserved that good thing. And that Abby did, too.

Instead, he pulled her to a stop at the top of the stairs, just before the entrance to the club. He made the mistake of looking down, then closed his eyes in defense against that damn spinning.

"Do you ever plan on telling me?"

"What?"

"Vertigo. Was it a head injury? Is that why you left the SEALs?"

He drew a breath but looked at her. "Yes."

He could see that she was waiting for more, but what more was there? He'd told her. That should be enough. He didn't need to lay it on the ground for her; he'd already revealed that he wasn't the man he'd held himself out to be.

But she didn't say anything. Instead, she just took his hand and led him to the far side of the landing so they were away from the view. The world realigned, and his pulse slowed.

They were standing in front of the door to Masque, but that wasn't the elephant in the room.

"I'm not your dad," she finally said, lifting her shoulder.

He started to ask what she meant; started to pretend to misunderstand. But he *did* understand. She'd seen through to the core of him, just like she used to when they were kids. And she was telling him that she didn't care about his flaws. That unlike his father, she wouldn't give up on him.

He drew a breath, surprised that her quick understanding didn't make him feel vulnerable. But it didn't. It made him feel loved.

He met her eyes, then shrugged. "I guess that's a good thing. My dad would look terrible in that dress."

Her smile lit her eyes. "Yeah. He really would."

He cocked his head toward the door. "Are you sure? We don't have to. There's no reason on earth you need to feel like you have to one-up Francesca."

"It's not about that," she said.

His brows rose.

"No, really. It's not."

"Then what?"

She lifted a shoulder, looking embarrassed. "I want to know what other women have had with you. Not Francesca particularly. But I want what they've had. You don't want a relationship, well fine. But then I think it's fair that I get to know what it's like to be with the guy who fucks around."

Her words weren't said with a harsh tone, but he still heard it in his head. Because Abby wasn't part of that group. She was different. Special.

He almost told her so. Almost said they'd blow Masque off altogether.

Except he didn't. Because he wanted her there.

Mostly, he realized, he just wanted *her.*

"All right," he said, then led her to the door and showed his key. The door opened, and they were admitted to the party within the party.

He watched her face, taking in the couples talking, kissing, fucking. The main room was active tonight, and he knew the dungeon rooms would be even more so.

"What you expected?"

"I didn't know what to expect. Are we staying in here? Is there more?"

"We're staying," he said, noting how prominent her nipples were and the flush on her lips and cheeks. She was turned on. *Good.* Because he wanted her—and soon—but he didn't want to stay if she was uncomfortable.

Abby, however, seemed fine. A little awed, but fine. So he took her hand and led her to a nearby sofa, just as he had in his fantasy.

"Here," he said.

"Here? Here, what, exactly?"

"I guess we'll see," he said, unfastening his slacks and freeing his cock before he sat. "But why don't we start with you riding me?"

Her eyes were wide but excited, and he felt himself go harder knowing that this was really happening.

"Has *she* done that?"

He tilted his head, wondering about the jealousy. Liking it more than he should. "She has."

Abby's eyes narrowed. "Her skirt pulled up as she worked herself on you, everything nice and hidden by the flair of the material, but the whole room knowing exactly what you were doing?"

"Exactly."

"But they couldn't know for sure. It could be a ploy. She could have just been rubbing herself on you."

"True." He had no idea where she was going with this.

"That's not for me," she said, and he felt the disappointment cut through him like a knife. "If I'm claiming you—if I'm being claimed—I want everyone to know."

She looked around, at the same time reaching her hand back and unzipping her dress. He practically swallowed his tongue when she let the dress fall to the ground, and his cock got ten times harder when he looked at her, completely naked except for her shoes, a garter belt, and silk stockings.

Around them, most everyone had turned to watch, and he saw more than one guy's hand go to his own cock, stroking as he eyed Renly's girl.

He made a low noise in his throat. Not a growl, but pretty damn close.

She didn't look around at all. Instead, with her chin high, she came to him, not saying a single word. Then she took his hand and placed it between her thighs, arching back as he stroked her slick pussy.

She continued, her eyes never leaving his as she climbed onto the sofa, put both hands on his shoulders, and straddled him. He was rock hard. Painfully hard. And as she squirmed over the tip of his cock it was a wonder he didn't lose it right then.

But then—oh, God, then—she took his cock all the way, started to rock...and proceeded to completely blow his fucking mind.

# Chapter Twelve

They didn't say much on the ride back to her place, but as far as Renly was concerned, the soft touches and heated looks said everything, and the moment they stepped over her threshold and shut the door, he pulled her to him.

The kiss was slow and lingering. Tender and intimate. The direct opposite of their wild passion in Masque, but so much more compelling. And when they broke apart, both breathing hard, he led her into the bedroom, then lost himself in her arms. The scent of her. The feel of her. And when they both exploded for the second time that night, she curled up beside him, her fingers tracing patterns on his bare chest.

"Thank you," she whispered.

"What for?"

"For letting me go a little wild."

He chuckled. "I like you wild."

"And for telling me about your vertigo," she added, meeting his eyes. "For bringing me back into your life. I've missed you so much."

He cupped her cheek. "Me, too. But I'm not going anywhere."

"Dubai," she said, and he nodded slowly.

"That's not me leaving. That's just me going to work."

"And you're here right now," she said, rolling over so that his arm was beneath her breasts and he was spooned against her.

"Yeah," he whispered. "I'm right here."

He held her close, then drifted off, and for the first time in a very long time, it felt as if every single thing was right with the world.

\* \* \* \*

The next morning, they arrived ten minutes before Abby was supposed to meet Darrin, but he was already standing in the elevator bay when they reached Abby's office.

"Hey, Darrin," she said to the dark-haired man. "This is my friend Renly. We've got some plans for the rest of the day, so he's going to take care of some phone calls and emails while we work."

She unlocked the office door and led them all inside.

"No problem," Darrin said, speaking to Abby and barely acknowledging Renly. Either the guy was shy or an asshole. Right now he didn't know enough to make the call.

Once inside, Renly walked the perimeter of the office and checked in all the individual areas. Better safe than sorry. Abby and Darrin settled in the conference room, and Renly parked himself at the far end of the long table, planning to check his emails while they worked.

He lifted his head before he dove in, catching Darrin's eye. "I hope you don't mind if I hang out here. I don't know a damn thing about the tech world, and Abby said I could sit in and pretend to be fascinated."

Darrin's smile looked a little forced, but he said, "Sure. Don't know if you'll find it that fascinating, but I don't have a problem with it."

Renly gave him a thumbs up and then went back to his phone. He half-listened as Abby went through the various features of the software, pride building in him as he heard her competent voice and her clean explanations. She was able get to the heart of complex issues and answered all of Darrin's questions in a way that anyone—even Renly, who knew next to nothing about computers—could understand.

Soon enough, her voice became a pleasant background noise, and he deleted at least a hundred emails, mostly spam, that had built up in his inbox.

Then he cringed, realizing he'd completely missed one from his mother almost three days ago.

He pulled up text messaging and shot her a note.

**You there?**

*Renly! Where have you been hiding?*

**Sorry I missed your email. Crazy week.**
**I figured you would have tried again if it was important?**
**What's up?**

*Can't a mom just email her son?*

**Some moms can. You always have an agenda.**

*Ha ha.*

He grinned. His mom wasn't one for over-communication. She tended to write when she had something to say, and that was pretty much it.

**Come on, what's going on?**

*Well, to be honest, I'm getting married again.*

He hesitated as he stared at the words, not sure what to say.

**Oh.**

*Tell me how you really feel...*

He shook his head, then stood and left the conference room because he just needed to move around.

He paced inside the lobby, Abby's worried frown as he'd stepped out of the room burnt into his mind. Hopefully in a few minutes he could tell her everything was okay.

**Listen, mom, I'm excited for you.**
**But unless you've been keeping the biggest secret in the world,**
 **you haven't been dating anybody.**
**Who the hell are you marrying?**

*Well, to be honest, we've been dating for years.*
*It's time to make it official*

**Who? Do I know him?**

*Sweetie, it's Elise.*

He stared at his phone.

Elise—or Aunt Elise—was his mother's best friend and had been since they'd moved to Houston. All through his high school years they'd been inseparable, and after Renly and Red had moved away, Elise had actually moved in. They got along so well, and although Renly couldn't imagine living with a roommate at his mother's age, he understood that his mom had gotten lonely.

At least, that was what he'd always believed. Now, with the news of his mom's engagement, he saw everything in a fresh light.

**Mom? Why didn't you ever tell us?**

*I don't know. But I'm telling you now.*

**I think it's great.**
**I love Elise. But why the wedding now?**
**You guys have been living together for years.**

*We should have the moment it was legal.*
*Better late than never. I don't want to wake up one day*
*and find out that something happened and*
*regret that we never made it official.*

**What's going to happen?**

*I shouldn't have to explain that to somebody*
*who fights bad guys for a living.*
*You never know what life has in store for you.*
*Think about my hearing. Things can change in an instant,*
*and I don't want to regret anything.*

**I get that.**

And he did. Abby was filling his mind. Her smile, her touch.

**Mom, I think it's really great.**

*You do?*

**Of course. When's the wedding?**

*We haven't decided. But I'll make sure that the date is clear with you and Red.*

*And Abby,* he thought. He knew that wasn't his mother's intention, but this conversation had shifted something inside him, changing the way he thought about her. The way he thought about *them.*

*I need to go. I was just running out the door when you texted. I love you baby.*

**I love you too mom.**
**Give Elise a hug for me.**
**Have you told Red?**

*No, not yet. But I will. It's my news. Can you keep a secret from your brother?*

**LOL. No. You know that.**
**But I'll do my best.**
**So hurry up and tell him.**
**:).**

*Love you bunches. Talk soon.*

And then the text chain stopped. He stood there for a minute shaking his head, wondering at the miracle of conversation. How one simple statement by somebody could change your entire perspective on the world.

He tucked his phone back into his pocket and went into the break room. Darrin was there, standing near the coffee machine. "Hey," he said. "You look happy."

Renly shrugged. "Just had an interesting conversation with my mom. I'm happy for her. How's it going on the software?"

"Abby ran back to her office to get something. And I thought I needed a caffeine hit. Can I make you one?"

"Sure. That would be terrific. I could use some caffeine myself."

His phone pinged, and he looked down to see Red's message.

> *Just got a text from mom.*
> *She's right, they should've*
> *done that a long time ago.*

**Agree. In a meeting. Talk later?**

His brother sent him back a thumbs up emoji, and Renly made a mental note to call him later that evening. They needed to figure out what to do for their mom. Maybe fly her and Elise to someplace exotic for a honeymoon?

"—to just set it on the table?"

Renly shook his head, realizing that Darrin had passed him a coffee. "Sorry about that. I was texting with my brother." He took a sip of the coffee, then another, as Darrin went back to the coffee maker.

"Abby wants decaf," Darrin said. "I don't see the point. If you're going to drink coffee, drink coffee."

Renly chuckled and took another sip, waiting with Darrin for Abby's cup to brew, and as he stood there, he felt the damn vertigo kick in again. This time with a vengeance.

*What the fuck?*

Why the hell was it starting now? He hadn't even moved.

He set the coffee cup down, took a step, and tumbled to the ground, his mind as unstable as his body, and nothing in the world quite making sense.

He looked up, confused, and saw Darrin drop something into Abby's coffee.

Darrin turned to him, the smile he flashed giving Renly chills.

He tried to move, tried to make the world stop spinning, but he couldn't do anything.

And as the world started to turn black around him, he saw Darrin take the doped coffee out of the break room and head back toward Abby.

# Chapter Thirteen

Thank God for adrenaline.

Between that and Renly's terror for Abby, he'd managed to get his phone out and speed dial Stark Security. There was a twenty-four-hour hotline for agents in trouble, and although he'd passed out before connecting to the operator, the hotline had served its purpose, and the call had been put out. The team had tracked his phone, found his location, and now a medic was treating him for the lingering effects of the sedative that Darrin had used on him.

They still didn't have the labs back, but the doctor was pretty sure it was some sort of custom mix with various sedatives combined with a low dose of Rohypnol. Renly knew that whatever it was, Darrin had used the same thing on Abby.

She wasn't in the office, and he knew damn well she wouldn't have left willingly. That bastard had taken her, and right now the only thing that was occupying his mind was getting her back. Figuring out where she was, getting her to safety, and then taking out the son of a bitch who did this to her.

Many of Stark Security's agents were away on other assignments, but everyone who was available was now gathered in the Fairchild and Partners Development office. Nikki and Damien were there too, Nikki pacing the hall as she spoke to the owners of Greystone-Branch. They were working the case as well, digging into their recent hire's background. Because Renly couldn't believe this was the first time Darrin had done something like this.

"Okay, thanks," he heard Nikki say.

She came in to the break room—now Command Central—and relayed that Bijan, one of Greystone's owners, had talked to Darrin's last employer.

Although they hadn't mentioned it when Bijan had called for a recommendation, he admitted now that Darrin had been let go because of harassment complaints from the female staff.

"So he's escalating," Winston said.

"Did he say anything that might help us locate her?" Renly asked.

Tony was already at Darrin's apartment, searching his place. So far he hadn't reported back.

Local law enforcement had been contacted, and a detective was on sight, working with the team. The LAPD had agreed to let Stark Security take point, but they had a team working in the field and were prepared to respond once Abby was located.

Mario was checking traffic cams, hoping to get lucky and parse out the route Darrin took with Abby. So far, he'd only been able to track them a few blocks away before losing the thread.

Leah, with whom Renly had worked the most in his short time at Stark Security, was on the phone with someone at the county, working a hunch. Now he watched as she paced the far side of the room.

So far, it didn't look like her hunch was playing out.

As for himself, Renly was feeling damn useless. His head was throbbing, and he didn't have a single goddamn clue as to where the son of a bitch had taken her.

Leah came over and took his hand. "Hang in there," she said. "We're going to get her back."

He wanted to believe her, but fear was clinging to him. He'd had so much in his life just ripped out of his hands, and he was desperately afraid that Abby was going to follow that pattern.

And why the hell had he told her he didn't want to be in a relationship? She had to be scared, and he wished that he'd told her everything in his heart, if only so she'd have that to cling to.

He thought about his mother and Elise. His mother had waited too damn long. Years too long. Hell, for that matter, so had Renly. He should have told Abby he loved her on his first night back.

What was there to think about? Why would he say he didn't want to have a relationship with her?

Because he was an idiot. Because he was so goddamn afraid of losing her that he'd never claimed her.

And now here he was, and losing her was a very real possibility. And he was fucking useless between the vertigo and the jackhammer pounding in his head in the wake of the damn drugs.

*Just get the fuck over it, Cooper. Quit feeling sorry for yourself and work the problem.*

He looked at Ryan. "We need to track down his family tree. See if anyone alive owns property. Or if he inherited something that he hasn't taken title of yet."

Ryan nodded, and Nikki, still on the phone, stepped in, her head cocked as she listened to them speaking. Then she held up a finger. "Bijan, let me ask you something," she said, her voice fading as she stepped back out into the hall again.

Renly followed, his forehead creased with a frown. Damien was in the hall as well, also on the phone, and he looked up when Nikki clutched his arm.

"No, that's perfect," she said. "We'll check it out. Yes, of course I'll keep you updated."

She turned and looked at Renly. "His uncle owns a building in the garment district. Greystone considered buying and renovating it for office space but decided not to. It's not much," she said, "but at least it's a lead."

\* \* \* \*

Renly stared at the building, the old, abandoned warehouse in the garment district. It was a small one, currently under renovations, and there was an ancient, rickety fire escape that ran up one side.

"Heat signature on the third floor," Leah said beside him.

"The main doors are locked tight," Ryan said. "We can blow them, but it'll take a while to do it silently. We don't want him to know we're coming."

Renly nodded slowly, taking it all in. He looked at the fire escape. At the places where it appeared to be coming loose from the brick. Just looking at it made the world tilt beneath him.

But he could do it. He took a step forward. He could man up, go up there, and get Abby. He had to.

Leah frowned at him. "You okay?"

"Just a little head swimming from the drugs." He felt nausea rise as he imagined being on that fire escape, the world tilting until he was parallel to the ground. Darrin taunting him.

He'd drugged Renly; he must have drugged Abby. What else was he capable of doing?

Renly knew the answer. *Anything.*

And if Renly fucked up, then he also up fucked up Abby's only chance. He drew in a breath. He needed to be the one in that room. He needed to be the one who got to her. He needed to be her knight in shining armor. Because goddammit, he knew that he couldn't live without her, and he needed to tell her as much.

But he also had to be smart, and that reality—the reality that he'd been trying to suppress since he left the SEALs—rose up in front of him. The hardest choice in his career.

He looked at Leah. "Can you give me a minute? I need to talk to Ryan."

"Sure. Of course."

He could tell that she was curious, but she was too much of a professional to ask. Beside him, Ryan finished speaking to a local SWAT officer, then turned his attention to Renly. "What's on your mind?"

"I can't go to Dubai, and I can't climb that ladder."

Ryan nodded slowly. "Vertigo?"

Renly took a step back. "You know?"

"I suspected. You told us about the head injury. I've seen you stumble a couple of times. And I can't think of any reason other than that that you wouldn't want to go up that ladder to rescue the woman you love."

Renly smiled. He hadn't told anyone he loved her, but it was nice to know that it showed. Hopefully that meant she knew, too.

"I'm an asshole. I should have told you a long time ago. I should have told you at least before you assigned me to Dubai. The type of operation that is, I'd be useless in the field."

"I think that's my call," Ryan said. "And you and I know there's a hell of a lot more to an operation than being the one who scales the outside of a building. That being said, under the circumstances, I don't think you really want to be rushing off to the Middle East and leaving Abby behind. I'll put you on something local, and you can stay here until your vertigo calms down and you and Abby are settled."

Renly stared at him. "You still want me on the team?"

To his surprise, Ryan laughed outright. "You're an excellent agent, Renly. And I'm going to assume you weren't listening to me when I told you that there's plenty you can do where your vertigo won't be an issue. I've known a lot of men with head injuries who developed vertigo, and it tends to calm down in time. You're going to be fine. I wish you'd told us, but you're going to be fine."

"Right. Good." Relief flooded him. Hope, too. The day was turning around, and that could only mean good things for their chances.

Ryan cleared his throat. "Of course, if you keep something like that from us again, we're going to have another talk, and I don't think you're going to like the outcome of that one. But right now, we're five by five."

Renly grinned. "In that case, I need to know who you're sending up. I need whoever you think is best in the field to go in and rescue my girl."

Ten minutes later, Emma was standing beside him. A former operative with a secret government agency, she was the best sharpshooter in Stark Security. "Don't worry," she said. "We'll get her back."

Renly nodded, hating the fact that he wasn't the one going up, but knowing this was about saving Abby, not making Renly feel warm and fuzzy.

The plan was for Emma to go up, assess the situation, and radio back. She'd take care of Darrin, and on her mark, the below team would blow the downstairs door.

When the team went in, Renly intended to be first in line. There'd still be stairs, but there'd be a solid wall and no outside world flipping sideways around him.

"Are you okay?" Emma said.

"Yeah," he said. "Take care of my girl."

"You'll have her back soon."

"I know." He still hated the fact that he wasn't on the front line, but for the first time in a long time, he'd been honest about who he was and what he was capable of.

And at the end of the day, it was that honesty that was going to ensure he got Abby back.

# Chapter Fourteen

I'm shaking, and I don't know if it's from the after-effects of whatever Darrin drugged me with or fear.

I think it's fear.

Although I'm shaking—and although I can't see a thing through the blindfold—I'm actually pretty clear-headed. I've been listening to the room, trying to figure out what Darrin is doing and where we are.

It's echoey, and I assume it's big. I have a vague memory of being carried upstairs. I don't know how long we've been here, and I don't know what's happened to Renly.

The last thing I remember is my head swimming and the world fading away. I'd been unable to move my legs or arms, but my eyes were open as we passed the break room, and I saw him sprawled there on the floor, spilled coffee all around him. My chest had tightened, but I couldn't do anything, not even call out.

Everything after that is a blur. Sounds and images. It could be days that I've been here. It could only be hours. I don't know. All I know is that I'm terrified for Renly. And for myself, too.

"Darrin?"

He makes a noise but doesn't answer.

"Darrin, please. Please at least take off the blindfold."

I hear the tread of his steps as he comes closer. And I feel hot breath on my face as he bends in close, the scent of onions surrounding me. "Why the hell do you think I would do you any favors, bitch? After the way you treated me? Do you really think you deserve to ask for anything?"

"I'm sorry if I treated you badly. I didn't understand how you felt. I wish you'd told me outright. I'm so flattered now that I know. I'd really love to get to know you better."

The lie makes me sick, but if it saves my life—if it gets me back to Renly—I'll pretty much say or do anything. "Please. Please just take the blindfold off so we can talk."

I hear squeaking outside, and I assume it's from a fire escape. He'd said something earlier about a warehouse. And I wonder where exactly we are. Downtown Los Angeles, probably, in one of the old districts where there are abandoned garment factories. But I don't know for certain. For all I know we're in another state by now.

"Please?" I try to reach out, but my arms are tied to a chair.

He bends closer, and I smell his breath again. I feel his fingers trace the outline of the blindfold. Then he steps back, and I hold my breath, expecting him to take the thing off. Instead he reaches out and slaps me hard across the cheek.

"Bitch." I hear him pacing in front of me. "Did you think I wouldn't see the way you were cheating on me? We had something special, and you just ignored it. You went to that club with that man. You did nasty things with him. You cheated on me. But you won't be doing anything else with him. I'll make sure of that."

Fear cuts through me, but there's hope as well. He's not talking as if Renly is dead. He's talking as if he will be, and that at least keeps hope alive.

"I told you, I didn't know how you felt. But I do now."

"What makes you think that I would want you now? I saw what you did with him. Right where anyone could see. Slut."

I almost beg again, but I don't want him to get more riled up. So instead I dip my head and say, "I'm sorry."

I'm searching for the magic words, but I don't know what they are. He comes closer, his hands going over mine, cupping me and the armrest to which I'm tied. He's right there. So close. If my legs were free, I could kick him in the balls.

"I don't want you anymore," he says. "Don't you get it? You're not here because I want to keep you. You're here because I'm going to toss you away. That's what you do with rotten things, isn't it?"

"Darrin, please."

He makes a rough sound that's almost like a growl, and I feel the chair move as he pushes roughly back from me, then feel the sharp sting of his hand against my cheek. I scream, and as I do, I hear a sharp crack. I have no idea what's going on, but there's a thud in front of me, and for a moment—one blissful moment—I think that Darrin has fallen.

*Renly?*

I don't dare to say it out loud. If I'm wrong—if Darrin isn't injured—he'd hurt me for that. He'd punish me for thinking of Renly.

But I have to know what's going on. I rock, trying to shake in the chair. And then I feel hands on my shoulders. "It's okay," a woman's voice says. "He's down, and you're safe."

"Emma?" A sob breaks free. "Oh God, Emma, where's Renly?"

"Abby, baby. I'm right here."

The voice is across the room, and I hear the pounding of footsteps as he races to me. And then someone is ripping off the blindfold, and Renly's right there in front of me, one hand on my thighs, his other cupping my head.

He pulls me close and kisses me hard, then leans back long enough to work on my bindings.

Emma's already managed to do some, and I blink, realizing there's more going on around me than just Renly's face in front of me.

The whole team from Stark Security is here, and I throw my now-free arms around Renly's neck as he pulls me up to my feet.

He clutches me close, holding me so tight I fear he's going to crack a rib. "I almost lost you. Christ, Abby, I could have lost you. I don't think I could live if I lost you."

"I knew you'd come," I tell him, and it's not just hyperbole. I did know. Every cell in my body knew that somehow Renly would save me.

"Never again," he says, holding my shoulders and looking at me hard.

I manage a thin laugh. "Yeah, I sure as hell hope not."

"No," he says. "You away from me. Never again. You're mine, Abby. Dammit, I need you."

I blink, confused, then shake my head. Around us, the Stark Security team is securing the scene and patching up Darrin as we await the police. But I barely notice the activity. I'm too focused on Renly. The fear on his face. The passion in his words. "You're going to have to say that again," I tell him.

"You and me," he says. "Forever. Call it a relationship because it is one. Call it friends with benefits, because you are the best friend I will ever have, and if you'll have me, the last lover I'll ever have, too."

My heart flutters, and my hand flies to my mouth. "Is this a proposal?"

"Yes. No. I don't know. Is it?"

I laugh. "No," I say, feeling giddy enough that I could float on air. "I want to date first. But why don't we call it a promise?"

"Baby, I will promise you the world if you want it."

I shake my head, then feel warm tears on my cheeks as he pulls me even closer. "God, Renly, don't you get it? I never wanted the world. All I've ever really wanted is you."

# Epilogue

*Six months later...*

"Mel, isn't Abby's ring stunning?" Jo Swift glances over her shoulder toward her husband, Mel, Red's co-owner in the distillery.

"Yeah, yeah, great ring," he says, his attention on his phone.

Jo rolls her eyes at me. "Don't be insulted. He's in the middle of negotiating some big deal with a hotel chain. Keeping his attention on anything other than that phone the last two days has been a piece of work. But as for me," she continues enthusiastically, "that is absolutely gorgeous."

"It really is," I say, feeling deliciously giddy.

"Did Renly pick it out?"

"He did. And it's perfect."

He's a few feet away, talking with Red, and I see Jo's eyes shift that way, a small smile playing at her mouth. Happiness for me, I assume, and I reach out, gratified when Renly takes my hand without even looking.

"I'm so happy for you both," she says, and though she looks toward her husband, I don't see the smile I would expect. On the contrary, it almost seems as if a shadow has fallen over her.

I squeeze Renly's hand, and he meets my eyes, the love I see reflected there filling the abyss that Jo's darkness has created inside me.

She gives me a hug, then turns away, pasting on a smile as she heads toward Mel.

"They're not our role model," Renly says, whispering in my ear.

I look up, surprised. "What? Who?"

He strokes my hair. "Do you really believe I don't know what you're thinking?"

I laugh. "Fair enough. They don't have a spark at all. I don't want that to happen to us."

"It won't. It can't." Gently, he tilts my chin up. "Take another look around."

I do, taking in all of our friends who've come to celebrate our engagement. Nikki and Damien, Ryan and Jamie, Linda and Winston, and so many more from my work, from Renly's Hollywood jobs, and from Stark Security.

"There's so much love around us," he whispers. "But none of that even matters. Because we have enough love between us to last an eternity. We're going to be great, baby."

"Going to be?" I say with a quick shake of my head. "Sweetheart, we already are."

\* \* \* \*

Don't miss Red's story in Ravaged With You.

\* \* \* \*

Also from 1001 Dark Nights and J. Kenner, discover Cherish Me, Tease Me, Indulge Me, Damien, Hold Me, Tame Me, Tempt Me, Justify Me, Caress of Darkness, Caress of Pleasure, and Rising Storm.

Sign up for the 1001 Dark Nights Newsletter
and be entered to win a Tiffany Key necklace.

There's a contest every month!

Go to www.1001DarkNights.com to subscribe.

**As a bonus, all subscribers can download
FIVE FREE exclusive books!**

# Discover 1001 Dark Nights Collection Eight

DRAGON REVEALED by Donna Grant
A Dragon Kings Novella

CAPTURED IN INK by Carrie Ann Ryan
A Montgomery Ink: Boulder Novella

SECURING JANE by Susan Stoker
A SEAL of Protection: Legacy Series Novella

WILD WIND by Kristen Ashley
A Chaos Novella

DARE TO TEASE by Carly Phillips
A Dare Nation Novella

VAMPIRE by Rebecca Zanetti
A Dark Protectors/Rebels Novella

MAFIA KING by Rachel Van Dyken
A Mafia Royals Novella

THE GRAVEDIGGER'S SON by Darynda Jones
A Charley Davidson Novella

FINALE by Skye Warren
A North Security Novella

MEMORIES OF YOU by J. Kenner
A Stark Securities Novella

SLAYED BY DARKNESS by Alexandra Ivy
A Guardians of Eternity Novella

TREASURED by Lexi Blake
A Masters and Mercenaries Novella

THE DAREDEVIL by Dylan Allen
A Rivers Wilde Novella

BOND OF DESTINY by Larissa Ione
A Demonica Novella

THE CLOSE-UP by Kennedy Ryan
A Hollywood Renaissance Novella

MORE THAN POSSESS YOU by Shayla Black
A More Than Words Novella

HAUNTED HOUSE by Heather Graham
A Krewe of Hunters Novella

MAN FOR ME by Laurelin Paige
A Man In Charge Novella

THE RHYTHM METHOD by Kylie Scott
A Stage Dive Novella

JONAH BENNETT by Tijan
A Bennett Mafia Novella

CHANGE WITH ME by Kristen Proby
A With Me In Seattle Novella

THE DARKEST DESTINY by Gena Showalter
A Lords of the Underworld Novella

*Also from Blue Box Press*

THE LAST TIARA by M.J. Rose

THE CROWN OF GILDED BONES by Jennifer L. Armentrout
A Blood and Ash Novel

THE MISSING SISTER by Lucinda Riley

# Discover More J. Kenner

## Cherish Me: A Stark Ever After Novella

My life with Damien has always been magical, and never more so than during the holidays, a time for us to celebrate the hardships we've overcome and the incredible gift that is our family. Over the years, he has both protected and cherished me. He has made my life more rich and full than I could ever have imagined.

This year, he's treating me and our daughters to a holiday in Manhattan. With parades and ice skating, toy displays and candies. And, most of all, with each other.

It's a wonderful gift, a trip I will always cherish. But this year, I'm the one with the surprise. And I can't wait to see the look of delight and awe when I finally share my secret with Damien.

But I'm terrified that when danger strikes, it will take a holiday miracle for me to even get the chance.

\* \* \* \*

## Tease Me: A Stark International Novel

Entertainment reporter Jamie Archer knew it would be hard when her husband, Stark Security Chief Ryan Hunter, was called away for a long-term project in London. The distance is difficult to endure, but Jamie trusts the deep and passionate love that has always burned between them. At least until a mysterious woman from Ryan's past shows up at his doorstep, her very presence threatening to destroy everything that Jamie holds dear.

Ryan never expected to see Felicia Randall again, a woman with whom he shared a dark past and a dangerous secret. The first and only woman he ever truly failed.

Desperate and on the run, Felicia's come to plead for his help. But while Ryan knows that helping her is the only way to heal old wounds, he also knows that the mission will not only endanger the life of the woman he holds most dear, but will brutally test the deep trust that binds Jamie and Ryan together.

* * * *

## Indulge Me: A Stark Ever After Novella

Despite everything I have suffered, I never truly understood darkness until my family was in danger. Those desperate hours came close to breaking both Damien and me, but together we found the strength to survive and hold our family together.

Even so, my wounds are deep and wispy shadows still linger. But Damien is my rock. My hero against the dark and violence.

When dark memories threaten to consume me, he whisks me away, knowing that in order to conquer my fears he must take control. Demand my submission. Claim me completely. Because if I am going to find my center again, I must hold tight to Damien and draw deep from the wellspring of our shared passion.

* * * *

## Damien: A Stark Novel

I am Damien Stark. From the outside, I have a perfect life. A billionaire with a beautiful family. But if you could see inside my head, you'd know I'm as f-ed up as a person can be. Now more than ever.

I'm driven, relentless, and successful, but all of that means nothing without my wife and daughters. They're my entire world, and I failed them. Now I can barely look at them without drowning in an abyss of self-recrimination.

Only one thing keeps me sane—losing myself in my wife's silken caresses where I can pour all my pain into the one thing I know I can give her. Pleasure.

But the threats against my family are real, and I won't let anything happen to them ever again. I'll do whatever it takes to keep them safe— pay any price, embrace any darkness. They are mine.

I am Damien Stark. Do you want to see inside my head? Careful what you wish for.

* * * *

## Hold Me: A Stark Ever After Novella

My life with Damien has never been fuller. Every day is a miracle, and every night I lose myself in the oasis of his arms.

But there are new challenges, too. Our families. Our careers. And new responsibilities that test us with unrelenting, unexpected trials.

I know we will survive—we have to. Because I cannot live without Damien by my side. But sometimes the darkness seems overwhelming, and I am terrified that the day will come when Damien cannot bring the light. And I will have to find the strength inside myself to find my way back into his arms.

* * * *

## Justify Me: A Stark International/Masters and Mercenaries Novella

McKay-Taggart operative Riley Blade has no intention of returning to Los Angeles after his brief stint as a consultant on mega-star Lyle Tarpin's latest action flick. Not even for Natasha Black, Tarpin's sexy personal assistant who'd gotten under his skin. Why would he, when Tasha made it absolutely clear that—attraction or not—she wasn't interested in a fling, much less a relationship.

But when Riley learns that someone is stalking her, he races to her side. Determined to not only protect her, but to convince her that—no matter what has hurt her in the past—he's not only going to fight for her, he's going to win her heart. Forever.

* * * *

## Tame Me: A Stark International Novella

Aspiring actress Jamie Archer is on the run. From herself. From her wild child ways. From the screwed up life that she left behind in Los Angeles. And, most of all, from Ryan Hunter—the first man who has the potential to break through her defenses to see the dark fears and secrets she hides.

Stark International Security Chief Ryan Hunter knows only one thing for sure—he wants Jamie. Wants to hold her, make love to her, possess her, and claim her. Wants to do whatever it takes to make her his.

But after one night of bliss, Jamie bolts. And now it's up to Ryan to not only bring her back, but to convince her that she's running away from the best thing that ever happened to her--him.

* * * *

## Tempt Me: A Stark International Novella

Sometimes passion has a price...

When sexy Stark Security Chief Ryan Hunter whisks his girlfriend Jamie Archer away for a passionate, romance-filled weekend so he can finally pop the question, he's certain that the answer will be an enthusiastic yes. So when Jamie tries to avoid the conversation, hiding her fears of commitment and change under a blanket of wild sensuality and decadent playtime in bed, Ryan is more determined than ever to convince Jamie that they belong together.

Knowing there's no halfway with this woman, Ryan gives her an ultimatum – marry him or walk away. Now Jamie is forced to face her deepest insecurities or risk destroying the best thing in her life. And it will take all of her strength, and all of Ryan's love, to keep her right where she belongs...

* * * *

## Caress of Darkness: A Dark Pleasures Novella

From the first moment I saw him, I knew that Rainer Engel was like no other man. Dangerously sexy and darkly mysterious, he both enticed me and terrified me.

I wanted to run—to fight against the heat that was building between us—but there was nowhere to go. I needed his help as much as I needed his touch. And so help me, I knew that I would do anything he asked in order to have both.

But even as our passion burned hot, the secrets in Raine's past reached out to destroy us ... and we would both have to make the greatest sacrifice to find a love that would last forever.

Don't miss the next novellas in the Dark Pleasures series!

Find Me in Darkness, Find Me in Pleasure, Find Me in Passion, Caress of Pleasure...

* * * *

Storm, Texas.

Where passion runs hot, desire runs deep, and secrets have the power to destroy...

Nestled among rolling hills and painted with vibrant wildflowers, the bucolic town of Storm, Texas, seems like nothing short of perfection.

But there are secrets beneath the facade. Dark secrets. Powerful secrets. The kind that can destroy lives and tear families apart. The kind that can cut through a town like a tempest, leaving jealousy and destruction in its wake, along with shattered hopes and broken dreams. All it takes is one little thing to shatter that polish.

Rising Storm is a series conceived by Julie Kenner and Dee Davis to read like an on-going drama. Set in a small Texas town, Rising Storm is full of scandal, deceit, romance, passion, and secrets. Lots of secrets.

# Cherish Me
### A Stark Ever After Novella
### By J. Kenner
### Now available

My life with Damien has always been magical, and never more so than during the holidays, a time for us to celebrate the hardships we've overcome and the incredible gift that is our family. Over the years, he has both protected and cherished me. He has made my life more rich and full than I could ever have imagined.

This year, he's treating me and our daughters to a holiday in Manhattan. With parades and ice skating, toy displays and candies. And, most of all, with each other.

It's a wonderful gift, a trip I will always cherish. But this year, I'm the one with the surprise. And I can't wait to see the look of delight and awe when I finally share my secret with Damien.

But I'm terrified that when danger strikes, it will take a holiday miracle for me to even get the chance.

\* \* \* \*

"Mommy! Daddy! Watch this! Watch this!"

I turn just in time to see Lara, my oldest, grab her little sister's hands. Both girls lean back, their eyes to the sky as they spin and spin and spin until finally, they let go and tumble into a dizzy heap on the play mat next to Dallas and Jane Sykes' massive swimming pool.

"Very nice," Damien says, shooting me a sideways grin as he squeezes my hand. It's four-thirty, and the setting sun casts a golden haze over the yard, making Damien's raven-black hair gleam.

"Can I spin and then jump in the pool?" Lara asks. "Pretty please?" She's five now, and convinced that she can do anything and everything without repercussions. Sometimes I think that might be true. She's Daddy's little girl, after all.

"No, you can't," I say, adjusting my blanket. I'm stretched out on a comfy outdoor sofa, my legs curled up so that my feet are just brushing Damien's thighs. Normally, he'd be resting one hand on my leg, but today he's cradling Mystery, Dallas and Jane's baby daughter, who's cooing sleepily in his arms.

"But Mommy!"

"Lara…" I put on my stern Mommy voice. "The pool is too cold, and you don't want to be sick for the rest of our trip, do you?"

"We won't get sick," Lara says. "I'm healthy as a horse. Grandpa said so."

I stifle a laugh, remembering the last time my father had hoisted Lara to his shoulders and said that exact thing.

"Please," Anne chimes in. At three, she happily follows her sister's lead. "Daddy, we wanna swim dizzy."

"Swim dizzy?" Jane asks as she returns to the pool deck with a tray of drinks. Her long, brown hair is pulled back into a messy ponytail, but a few strands curl around her face. "We've got regular cider for the kids and wine or bourbon for the grownups. Dallas'll be out in a few with some snacks. Until then, I'm dying to know what your kids are talking about."

She sets the tray down on the table in front of the sofa, meets my eyes, and passes me a wine glass sitting atop a napkin. I give her a quick, shared smile as Damien starts to explain.

"Laura discovered the joys of getting dizzy, then jumping into the pool with her eyes closed this summer." His smile reaches his dual-colored eyes, the corners crinkling in a way that I find wonderfully sexy. "I tried it, too, and I have to say she has a point."

I shake my head in mock exasperation, but I do understand the appeal. The sensation of being totally helpless and disoriented. The thrill of conquering all of that as you get your bearings, and the world rights itself again.

I'd been nervous when Lara first discovered this new "game," but the kid is part fish. More than that, she follows the rules we've set for our pool back in Malibu. Only one dizzy swim per outing. And never, ever in the pool without an adult. Not that they could get through the child protective locks that guard the now-fenced pool area. Or, for that matter, the various alarms, cameras, and other security alert systems that Damien has installed. Some of which are newly patented designs conceived by Damien post-fatherhood and now being produced and marketed under the Stark Applied Technology umbrella.

Whatever it takes to keep our girls safe.

"I'll have to try that," Jane says, sliding into one of the chairs opposite me and Damien. "I didn't even think about heating the pool for the girls. Today would have been a great day for it."

We've come to New York for the Christmas holidays, and although we're moving on to the city tomorrow, we're spending tonight here with our friends at their incredible Southampton mansion on the street known by the media as Billionaire's Row.

This particular home is often described as the icing on the Meadow Lane cake. Once, it had been notorious as the home of The King of Fuck, the billionaire playboy. But Dallas Sykes, who had encouraged that nickname for reasons of his own, is a man who'd lived a hidden life. A serious man behind the disguise of a lazy heir content to plow through a seemingly never-ending supply of dollars.

I once thought I'd grown up wealthy in my fine Texas neighborhood, but after I met Damien, I'd learned what the word really meant. I've become acclimated to the kinds of homes that fill the pages of magazines. But even to my now-acclimated vision, the Sykes' mansion shines bright.

Originally their childhood home, it now belongs to Jane and Dallas as husband and wife. An admittedly odd situation, considering they grew up as siblings, and one that the press had been all over a few years ago. But it makes sense, and I couldn't be happier for the two of them. Especially since I couldn't imagine Dallas or Jane without the other anymore than I could imagine me without Damien.

We arrived just before lunch, and this day and tomorrow morning are all about relaxing and catching up. Tomorrow, we're leaving the girls with Dallas and Jane, then heading into the city for one night of kid-free alone time. It's the part of the trip that I've taken full charge of—finding the hotel, setting up reservations under a fake name so that we will be totally anonymous, buying the lingerie I intend to wear—or not—when we're alone.

Damien's fully in on that aspect of the itinerary. What he doesn't know is that I have a special gift that I plan to give him during our dinner tomorrow before we head back to the room.

# About J. Kenner

J. Kenner (aka Julie Kenner) is the *New York Times, USA Today, Publishers Weekly, Wall Street Journal* and #1 International bestselling author of over one-hundred novels, novellas and short stories in a variety of genres.

JK has been praised by *Publishers Weekly* as an author with a "flair for dialogue and eccentric characterizations" and by *RT Bookclub* for having "cornered the market on sinfully attractive, dominant antiheroes and the women who swoon for them."

In her previous career as an attorney, JK worked as a lawyer in Southern California and Texas. She currently lives in Central Texas, with her husband, two daughters, and two rather spastic cats.

Visit JK online at www.jkenner.com
Subscribe to JK's Newsletter
Text JKenner to 21000 to subscribe to JK's text alerts
Twitter
Instagram
Facebook Page
Facebook Fan Group

# Discover 1001 Dark Nights

TANGLED by Rebecca Zanetti ~ HOLD ME by J. Kenner ~ SOMEHOW, SOME WAY by Jennifer Probst ~ TOO CLOSE TO CALL by Tessa Bailey ~ HUNTED by Elisabeth Naughton ~ EYES ON YOU by Laura Kaye ~ BLADE by Alexandra Ivy/Laura Wright ~ DRAGON BURN by Donna Grant ~ TRIPPED OUT by Lorelei James ~ STUD FINDER by Lauren Blakely ~ MIDNIGHT UNLEASHED by Lara Adrian ~ HALLOW BE THE HAUNT by Heather Graham ~ DIRTY FILTHY FIX by Laurelin Paige ~ THE BED MATE by Kendall Ryan ~ NIGHT GAMES by CD Reiss ~ NO RESERVATIONS by Kristen Proby ~ DAWN OF SURRENDER by Liliana Hart

COLLECTION FIVE
BLAZE ERUPTING by Rebecca Zanetti ~ ROUGH RIDE by Kristen Ashley ~ HAWKYN by Larissa Ione ~ RIDE DIRTY by Laura Kaye ~ ROME'S CHANCE by Joanna Wylde ~ THE MARRIAGE ARRANGEMENT by Jennifer Probst ~ SURRENDER by Elisabeth Naughton ~ INKED NIGHTS by Carrie Ann Ryan ~ ENVY by Rachel Van Dyken ~ PROTECTED by Lexi Blake ~ THE PRINCE by Jennifer L. Armentrout ~ PLEASE ME by J. Kenner ~ WOUND TIGHT by Lorelei James ~ STRONG by Kylie Scott ~ DRAGON NIGHT by Donna Grant ~ TEMPTING BROOKE by Kristen Proby ~ HAUNTED BE THE HOLIDAYS by Heather Graham ~ CONTROL by K. Bromberg ~ HUNKY HEARTBREAKER by Kendall Ryan ~ THE DARKEST CAPTIVE by Gena Showalter

COLLECTION SIX
DRAGON CLAIMED by Donna Grant ~ ASHES TO INK by Carrie Ann Ryan ~ ENSNARED by Elisabeth Naughton ~ EVERMORE by Corinne Michaels ~ VENGEANCE by Rebecca Zanetti ~ ELI'S TRIUMPH by Joanna Wylde ~ CIPHER by Larissa Ione ~ RESCUING MACIE by Susan Stoker ~ ENCHANTED by Lexi Blake ~ TAKE THE BRIDE by Carly Phillips ~ INDULGE ME by J. Kenner ~ THE KING by Jennifer L. Armentrout ~ QUIET MAN by Kristen Ashley ~ ABANDON by Rachel Van Dyken ~ THE OPEN DOOR by Laurelin Paige~ CLOSER by Kylie Scott ~ SOMETHING JUST LIKE THIS by Jennifer Probst ~ BLOOD NIGHT by Heather Graham ~ TWIST OF FATE by Jill Shalvis ~ MORE THAN PLEASURE YOU by Shayla Black ~ WONDER WITH ME by Kristen Proby ~ THE DARKEST ASSASSIN by Gena Showalter

COLLECTION SEVEN
THE BISHOP by Skye Warren ~ TAKEN WITH YOU by Carrie Ann Ryan ~ DRAGON LOST by Donna Grant ~ SEXY LOVE by Carly Phillips ~ PROVOKE by Rachel Van Dyken ~ RAFE by Sawyer Bennett ~ THE

NAUGHTY PRINCESS by Claire Contreras ~ THE GRAVEYARD SHIFT by Darynda Jones ~ CHARMED by Lexi Blake ~ SACRIFICE OF DARKNESS by Alexandra Ivy ~ THE QUEEN by Jen Armentrout ~ BEGIN AGAIN by Jennifer Probst ~ VIXEN by Rebecca Zanetti ~ SLASH by Laurelin Paige ~ THE DEAD HEAT OF SUMMER by Heather Graham ~ WILD FIRE by Kristen Ashley ~ MORE THAN PROTECT YOU by Shayla Black ~ LOVE SONG by Kylie Scott ~ CHERISH ME by J. Kenner ~ SHINE WITH ME by Kristen Proby

Discover Blue Box Press
TAME ME by J. Kenner ~ TEMPT ME by J. Kenner ~ DAMIEN by J. Kenner ~ TEASE ME by J. Kenner ~ REAPER by Larissa Ione ~ THE SURRENDER GATE by Christopher Rice ~ SERVICING THE TARGET by Cherise Sinclair ~ THE LAKE OF LEARNING by Steve Berry and MJ Rose ~ THE MUSEUM OF MYSTERIES by Steve Berry and MJ Rose ~ TEASE ME by J. Kenner ~ FROM BLOOD AND ASH by Jennifer L. Armentrout ~ QUEEN MOVE by Kennedy Ryan ~ THE HOUSE OF LONG AGO by Steve Berry and MJ Rose ~ THE BUTTERFLY ROOM by Lucinda Riley ~ A KINGDOM OF FLESH AND FIRE by Jennifer L. Armentrout

## On Behalf of 1001 Dark Nights,

Liz Berry, M.J. Rose, and Jillian Stein would like to thank ~

Steve Berry
Doug Scofield
Benjamin Stein
Kim Guidroz
Social Butterfly PR
Ashley Wells
Asha Hossain
Chris Graham
Chelle Olson
Kasi Alexander
Jessica Johns
Dylan Stockton
Richard Blake
and Simon Lipskar

Made in the USA
Monee, IL
18 October 2021